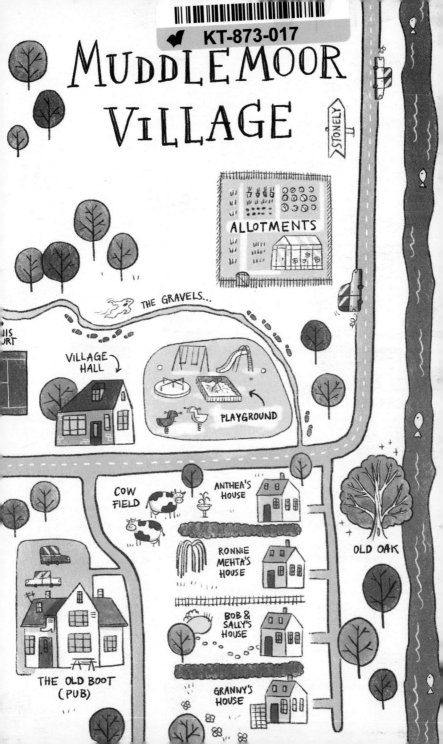

For Bea, Arthur, John, Rosie, Maria,
William, Louis, Zach and Stella –
cousins and comrades xx
– R.Q.

For my husband James,
with all my love xx
– M.K

First published in 2022 by
Andersen Press Limited
20 Vauxhall Bridge Road
London SW1V 2SA
Vijverlaan 48, 3062 HL Rotterdam, Nederland
www.andersenpress.co.uk

2 4 6 8 10 9 7 5 3 1

British Library Cataloguing in Publication Data available.

ISBN 978 1 83913 127 1
Printed and bound in Great Britain by Clays Ltd, Elcograf S.p.A.

THE
MUDDLEMOOR
MYSTERIES

THE
BOOK
CLUB
BANK
HEIST

by Ruth Quayle

illustrated by
Marta Kissi

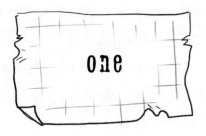

I f someone in your family joins a book club, make sure you keep an eye on them because book clubs are not always what they seem.

The reason I know this is because in the Easter holidays, when me and my cousins, Tom and Pip Berryman, were staying with our granny in the countryside without our parents, we discovered something SUSPICIOUS about Granny's book club.

Our granny's village

GRANNY

is called Muddlemoor and even though it looks quiet and safe it is actually REALLY DANGEROUS. Bad things are always happening in Muddlemoor and they ALWAYS seem to happen in the school holidays when me, Tom and Pip are staying there.

Like for instance, last summer we discovered that Granny's best friend, Anthea, had invented a dangerous robot spy cat to spy on Granny so that she could steal Granny's secret chocolate fudge cake recipe and win the Great Village Bake Off.

We spent AGES solving that mystery, and we even had to kidnap the robot spy cat to stop it spying on Granny, but in the end Anthea got away with EVERYTHING as she is cleverer than most people.

I hadn't seen Tom and Pip much since then – only at Christmas when their whole family came to London to go to the pantomime. (Mainly Tom and Pip live in Wales which is a long way from my flat in London). But going to the pantomime in London wasn't the same as being together at Granny's because our parents were there

JOE ROBINSON

and there wasn't a mystery to solve.

In case you don't know me, I am Joe Robinson and I am nine and one quarter. Mainly people think I am younger than nine because I am on the small side and I sometimes suck my fingers.

My teachers are always ordering me to brush my hair and tuck in my shirt. They say, 'What ARE we going to do with you, Joe Robinson?' in a sighing sort of voice. This is probably because I am not very speedy at maths or literacy but I am quite good at catching balls, except really high ones, and I am REALLY GOOD at making up games to play at break time. Mum says I have an A* imagination and she also says that having a good imagination is as important as maths and literacy. But I think she might be fibbing because she is my mum and it is her job to say I am clever.

My cousins Tom and Pip are PROPERLY clever – cleverer than most people (except for their dad, my Uncle Marcus, who is a brain box). Tom and Pip are also really brave and confident. You would not necessarily guess

TOM AND PIP

about them being brave and confident if you met them at, e.g. a birthday party or at a football match, but if you knew them as well I as do, you would understand what I mean. Tom reads everything he can get his hands on and Pip is calm in a crisis. Tom and Pip are better than all the children in my school put together, including Jack Passmore. This is why it is ESPECIALLY lucky that we get to see each other when we stay at Granny's during the holidays.

Our parents do not realise about most of the things we get up to when we are staying at Granny's. We try not to tell them because if they knew even half of it, they might stop us going. Luckily Granny doesn't spill the beans to our parents because, even though Granny is keen on telling the truth, she isn't one of life's tell-tales.

My sister Bella (who is at university) says there is nothing to do in Muddlemoor. But Bella is wrong because, even though Granny doesn't live near a beach or a theme park and even though she doesn't have many toys in her cottage (apart from some Lego that used to belong to Mum and Uncle Marcus when they were our age), me, Tom and Pip never get bored when we are staying with her, not even when it's raining.

That's because at Granny's we have to keep our wits about us AT ALL TIMES. That's just something you have to put up with if your granny lives in a dangerous neighbourhood.

Once I told Granny that she is lucky to have us around to keep her safe, but when I said this her eyes went all crinkly and she said, 'Keep me on my toes more like' and then she got the hysterics.

Granny gets the hysterics all the time because she thinks a lot of things in life are funny, even stuff that most grown-ups think are serious.

But at the end of the Easter holidays, Granny did not get the giggles until right at the end. First of all she was quite cross and then she got a bit worried and then she was really cross all over again.

But we didn't mind as much as we normally would because even though we prefer it when Granny is NOT cross, we weren't actually sorry about what we had done. Deep down, we were RELIEVED that we had been around to keep an eye on Granny because, the thing is, she needed us. As you're about to find out.

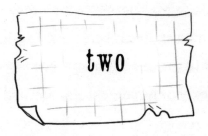

two

At the start of the holidays I was late getting to Granny's because Mum's car broke down just after we set off from our flat in London. Luckily, Mum knew what the problem was – there were loads of leaves stuck in the car's exhaust pipe because Mum always parks it under a half-dead sycamore tree. Mum said that when a car's exhaust is blocked, the engine won't work.

Mum and I spent ages on the side of the road pulling out all the mushy leaves with our fingers, but eventually the car started and we managed to drive all the way to Granny's without stopping.

By the time we'd arrived and taken the bags out of the car and eaten a Jaffa cake, it was nearly lunch time.

Mum and Uncle Marcus told Granny they were going to stay for a quick lunch before driving home. Mum and Uncle Marcus think Granny's cooking is the best on the planet because she is their mum and they grew up eating it.

As soon as lunch started, Uncle Marcus started talking. When Uncle Marcus starts talking it can get quite boring because he is a know-it-all and likes to tell you everything he knows in one helping. Me, Tom and Pip gobbled down our spaghetti Bolognese really quickly because we hadn't seen each other for ages and we wanted to leave the table as soon as possible to get away from the grown-ups. But Uncle Marcus and Mum were having a discussion about the prime minister and it slightly turned into an argument because Mum and Uncle Marcus get into arguments about most topics of conversation, especially the prime minister.

When Mum and Uncle Marcus argue none of us can get a word in edgeways which is unusual for me because I am known for being a chatterbox (except I prefer talking about the FA Cup or how to make slime).

In the end, I interrupted to ask if we could leave the table because we had finished our lunch, but Uncle Marcus said that it was good for children to be involved in adult conversation. Tom pointed out that we weren't exactly involved in the conversation because he (Uncle Marcus) was doing most of the talking, but Uncle Marcus just laughed and asked Granny and Mum what they thought about the state of the economy.

It turned out to be the longest lunch EVER, even longer than the lunch in the posh restaurant Mum won vouchers for at the school summer fair, when we had to eat nine courses without a break, and I wasn't allowed to sit on my knees because my trainers were a bit muddy and the chairs were covered in white silk.

But, FINALLY, when the grown-ups were drinking coffee, Uncle Marcus said we could leave the table as

long as we went upstairs and unpacked our bags. We raced straight upstairs, but we didn't unpack our bags because unpacking is not our favourite thing to do in life and also it is not important. Plus, we had too much to chat about.

Tom and Pip told me about a really strict new teacher at their school called Mr Evans who carried a black walking stick even though he didn't have a limp. Tom said all the children at their school were really scared of Mr Evans because when Mr Evans got cross he waved his stick around in the air and, once, Mr Evans's stick hit Pip's little finger by accident. Pip's mum (my aunt Polly) reported it to their head teacher – and now Mr Evans leaves his black stick in his car in the school car park and pretend limps everywhere.

I was just thinking how glad I was that I didn't go to Tom and Pip's school and have Mr Evans as a teacher when Mum and Uncle Marcus called up the stairs and told us they were leaving. Luckily, I never mind saying goodbye to Mum when I am staying at Granny's because when you have a granny and cousins to keep you company it is hard to feel homesick. We went out to Little Draycott (which is the name of Granny's road) and waved goodbye as Mum and Uncle Marcus drove away.

'Good,' said Tom. 'That's better.' And I knew exactly what Tom meant because even though I really love my mum, it is nicer when it is just me and my cousins at Granny's.

As we walked down Little Draycott, Tom told us about a new series of books he was reading about a boy called Albie Short who is an amazing detective. He showed us the front cover of a book he had in his back pocket. It was of a boy with black hair and freckles holding a map. Tom told us there were three books in the series, *Gotcha!*, *Trapped!* and *Target!*, and he had already read them all twice.

'Albie Short and I share a common outlook,' said Tom.

Pip did a backflip and I told her that it was really good. Straightaway Pip stopped doing backflips and stared at her shoes.

'Pip has gone off doing gymnastics in front of people,' explained Tom. 'She doesn't like the attention.'

'I don't mind if it's just you and Tom,' said Pip apologetically. 'I just hate it when strangers – mainly adults – ask me to perform in front of them.'

Pip shrugged her shoulders and I could tell that she was a bit embarrassed so, to change the subject, I told them about when Dylan Moynihan cheated in the school cross country race by taking a short cut and how, when Mrs Vukovitch told Dylan he was disqualified, Dylan shouted, 'I've been robbed!' and pushed Kane Ashfield into some mud. But just when I was getting to the best bit (i.e. when Dylan Moynihan told Mrs Vukovitch she was a 'loser'), Tom interrupted and said, 'Vicar alert!' and pointed at a tall man with fluffy hair.

I stopped talking and looked at the vicar and noticed that he was peering through Ronnie Mehta's letterbox. (Ronnie Mehta lives a couple of doors down from Granny, on the other side of Bob and Sally Merry.)

Tom told us to duck behind the biggest oak tree on Little Draycott. The vicar turned round and I think he must have spotted my red T-shirt because he stopped looking from side to side and waved in our direction.

'School holidays, is it?'

Tom and Pip didn't say anything but I am not keen on silence so I said, 'We're here for nine days on our own because our parents have to work and we don't like going to holiday clubs if we can help it.'

The vicar laughed. 'I'd better be on my guard then,' he said. 'I've heard that you lot are sticklers for good behaviour.'

Tom took a sharp breath and said, 'Are you looking for Ronnie Mehta?'

The vicar grinned. 'Yes, I'm after his money!'

I think the vicar must have noticed our shocked

faces because he said: 'Actually I've mislaid something that I think I may have left here yesterday. Scatterbrain that I am.'

We nodded because one thing everyone knows is that the vicar is a forgetful person.

'Yes, but I'm also collecting money for the church roof which needs fixing and is going to cost a fortune to repair. That's why I'm out with my begging bowl – well, bucket – again. Except nobody seems to be home today. Maybe they're all avoiding me!'

The vicar slapped me on the back to show he was joking, but I could not laugh because being slapped on the back isn't very funny.

'What about you lot?' he asked. 'Any money to help pay for a new church roof?'

The vicar jangled his bucket and we looked at each other, all worried. We did have some money of our own, but we definitely DIDN'T want to spend it on a new church roof. We wanted to spend it on sweets.

'Ten pence here, twenty pence there,' said the vicar. 'Every little helps, as they say.'

He looked down at his mostly empty bucket of money and smiled. I put my hand into my jeans' pocket and felt the collection of coins. I knew exactly how much was there – fifty-four pence. I did a quick calculation in my head. If I gave the vicar ten pence I wouldn't have enough for a Chomp AND a Refresher bar in Mrs Rooney's shop.

'It leaked like billy-o last winter with all that rain. We had to leave buckets up and down the church aisle. Mrs Holgate nearly broke her hip when she tripped over one of them on her way to arrange the church flowers.'

The vicar turned to go. I glanced at Pip and Tom but they would not look at me. They were too busy staring at the laces on their trainers.

'Right-o. Better keep searching. Bye then.'

At that moment I did something a bit stupid. I put my hand in my pocket and pulled out what I thought was ten pence but was actually twenty pence.

'Here you go,' I said, flinging the twenty-pence coin into the vicar's bucket. I did not dare look at Tom and Pip's faces.

'Good man,' said the vicar. 'Much obliged.' Then he strolled back up Little Draycott and turned left onto the main road. We could hear him humming even when he was out of sight.

'You've been robbed,' said Tom.

'I know.'

'He basically guilt-tripped you into giving him the money.'

'Is that illegal?'

'No,' said Tom. 'But it's something to look out for next time. Vicars are obsessed with church roofs. You need to learn to avoid getting in long conversations like that.'

I nodded. I was not sure Tom was right about vicars being obsessed with church roofs, but I did NOT like the way the vicar had hoodwinked me into giving him twenty pence. When it came to that vicar we needed to keep an eye on our pocket money.

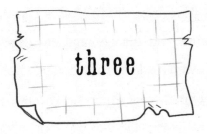

three

Three days went by and we didn't spot ANYTHING suspicious. No ghosts, no spies, no one trying to poison us – and no vicar after our money.

So we got on with doing the usual things instead. We found the Lego box and we played football in the garden and we hung out in Ronnie Mehta's weeping willow tree, which has branches all the way down to the ground.

The weeping willow tree is our favourite place to go when we have something important to discuss, and it's also where we keep things we don't want the grown-ups to find, e.g. bubble gum and a rusty pen knife. We keep them in a locked-up tin and Pip wears the key around her neck. No one knows we use the weeping willow as our hiding place except for maybe Ronnie Mehta and his teenage daughters, but they aren't interested because they don't go in their garden if they can help it.

Sometimes we mooched in the village because mooching is more interesting than it sounds. Like for instance we walked up to Mrs Rooney's shop to buy sweets and we played on the old tennis court next to the village hall.

It was fun but it wasn't as good as having a true-life crime to solve. Tom told us that we shouldn't get complacent (which means taking our eye off the ball) because, according to Albie Short, bad things always happen when you are least expecting them. But it was hard NOT to feel complacent because the truth was, nothing much was happening in Muddlemoor. It was even quieter than usual because lots of the people we knew, e.g. Sophie Pearce, were away on holiday.

Sophie Pearce is at secondary school and has a gold mobile phone. When she ISN'T away on holiday she is always taking the bus into Stonely to spend the money she earns from looking after people's chickens. Granny says that Sophie Pearce is a fearsome entrepreneur, but I don't find Sophie Pearce fearsome because she smiles a lot and is quite friendly. Then again, I think Tom might find her fearsome because he finds it tricky to speak to her.

The people who WERE in Muddlemoor weren't doing anything suspicious – not even Granny's friend Anthea who used to be a spy. Anthea is always asking us tricky questions and she likes to improve our education. Except we are not keen on improving our education, especially when it is the school holidays. Plus, we are not mad about Anthea because she smells of cats and always gets away with things.

Granny was acting normal too. She listened to the radio and watched *Cul-de-Sac* (which is her favourite programme on telly) and read the newspaper and filled up the bird feeders and she also did non-stop knitting. One day I asked her what she was knitting but she said it was a secret and she didn't want to spill the beans. I got a bit worried at this point because I thought she might be knitting something for ME to wear and I'm not one hundred per cent keen on Granny's knitted jumpers. But when Granny saw my face, she laughed and said, 'Don't worry, it's not for YOU,' and then she hid the pile of knitting in her knitting basket.

Compared to the last time we stayed with Granny, everything seemed very ordinary.

'Gosh,' said Granny on the morning of our fourth day. 'What on earth has happened to you lot? You're being UNUSUALLY WELL BEHAVED. Carry on like this and you may get through a whole visit without causing trouble.'

Granny laughed quite a lot when she said this and then she drove us to Sainsbury's to choose cheese and wine for her book club that evening.

Granny's book club meets up most weeks because, according to Anthea, they 'gobble up books like most people eat hot dinners'. Anthea is one of the regular members of Granny's book club, along with Bob Merry. (Bob comes on his own without his wife Sally because Sally takes their new puppy, Puff, for dog training classes on Thursday evenings.) The last member of Granny's book club is Mrs Mackintosh who is the strict head teacher of the primary school in Cudlington, the next-door village. We are quite scared of Mrs Mackintosh and we never call her by her first name (Janet) because head teachers don't suit first names. Very occasionally Ronnie Mehta comes along to book club too, but he doesn't have much time to read because he is always selling houses on his phone.

Granny says her book club is a weekly tonic. When I asked her what a tonic is she said, 'It's like a good dose of medicine for the soul.' This made me a bit worried because I didn't like the idea of Granny needing

Mrs Mackintosh

medicine for her soul. For one thing, I wasn't sure what a soul was. I thought it might be something to do with our feet but when I asked Granny, she said a soul isn't something you can see or touch. She says it is something that stays around after we are gone. Then she gave me a hug and went to prune the roses.

Granny's book club meets every Thursday evening and they always eat a lot of cheese and drink red wine. Even though they are all MAD ABOUT BOOKS Granny says they are not always mad about the SAME books. Sometimes they have arguments about the books they are reading. Granny says this is what makes a book club interesting. She says there's nothing worse than everybody being polite and agreeing with each other. Which is the complete opposite of what my teacher Mrs Vukovitch says whenever I have a fight with Ike Samuel. Mrs Vukovitch tells me and Ike Samuel that we need to learn to agree with each other. Except it is impossible to agree with Ike Samuel because he is a show-off. Also, he is wrong.

It was Granny's turn to host book club at her house so she chose about six different cheeses and lots of crackers, and a big tub of olives, and a few bottles of wine, and then she threw in a newspaper on top of all the things in her basket. I didn't look at that newspaper until we were waiting in the queue to pay, but waiting makes me a bit fidgety so I couldn't help glancing down at Granny's basket to see if she had put in any KitKats. (KitKats are our new favourite thing to eat.) That's when I read the headline on the front page of the newspaper and that's also when I got a big shock.

This is what it said:

I elbowed Tom and Pip and pointed to the newspaper and they both gasped so loudly that Granny looked up and raised her eyebrows.

I couldn't help gasping a bit too because Stonely is Granny's local town and we were in the Stonely Sainsbury's AT THAT MOMENT IN TIME.

'What on earth is the matter?' asked Granny.

I shook my head and gulped and Granny said, 'Good heavens,' and paid for the shopping.

I was suddenly REALLY CONCERNED because everybody knows that burglaries are a WORRY, especially when they are in the nearby town to where your granny lives.

Later on that day, after we'd unloaded the shopping and Granny had finished reading the newspaper, we took the article to our secret hiding place in Ronnie Mehta's weeping willow tree.

Tom had a squished pack of Fruit Pastilles in his pocket so we shared them out and then we read EVERYTHING about the masked robbers:

Masked thieves broke into a local hardware shop on Tuesday and terrorised shopkeeper Shirley Mason (53). The armed robbers raided Stonely Stores in broad daylight and made off with hundreds of pounds from the till. Ms Mason told police that there were five gang members and they were all wearing red balaclavas and carrying rucksacks. 'It was the most terrifying experience of my life,' she said. 'I'm still having flashbacks about those balaclavas.'

Stonely Stores is the third business in Stonely to be targeted by the gang in recent weeks. The other victims include Palamino Records and Rumsey's Coffee Shop. Police believe it is likely that the criminals will strike again.

PC Owen Shearcross said: 'We have reason to believe that this criminal gang is local to the area. Gang members may well be hiding in one of the smaller villages surrounding Stonely, planning their next robbery. They may be using a deserted building – for example an old shed – right in our midst. These criminals are armed and dangerous. We urge

members of the public NOT to approach them but to keep an eye out for any suspicious behaviour. If you have any information that may help us to arrest these criminals, please call our incidents team on: 07865 567433.

Me, Tom and Pip looked at each other and sucked a lot of air in through our teeth because when you are worried, sucking air through teeth is a helpful thing to do.

I could not stop thinking about Granny's jewellery collection that she hides in the laundry basket in the spare room. I had a feeling those armed robbers might be on their way to Granny's cottage to steal her jewellery RIGHT NOW.

We talked about Granny's trusting nature and then we talked about how Granny wasn't as young as she used to be. That's when we decided to be on the lookout because this gang of robbers could be hiding out in the countryside or in a rural village, e.g. Muddlemoor, right in front of our eyes. Plus, the police had asked members of the public, i.e. us, to keep an eye out for any suspicious behaviour.

For the rest of the day, we kept checking that Granny's doors and windows were closed and locked. This was quite tricky because Granny kept popping into the garden and leaving the back door wide open and when she was cooking our lunch she said, 'It's far too stuffy in here,' and flung open ALL the windows.

When she wasn't looking we shut all the windows and doors again, but in the end Granny got really fed up with us and told us we were getting in her way. So we had to leave her in danger for the rest of

the afternoon and go to the park. We sat underneath the zip wire and Tom took the first Albie Short book, *Gotcha!*, out of his back pocket.

'This is our reference book,' he said. 'It's about when Albie Short has to track down a gang of bank robbers on his own in broad daylight.'

I was really interested in hearing more about Albie Short so I stopped chatting and listened. I could tell Pip was listening too because she wasn't waggling her feet for once.

'Albie Short's trick,' said Tom, 'is to identify the key clues and focus on them. For example, in *Gotcha!* he speaks to all the people who have been robbed and EVERYBODY says that the robbers are covered

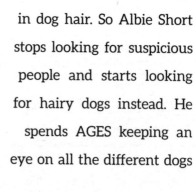

in dog hair. So Albie Short stops looking for suspicious people and starts looking for hairy dogs instead. He spends AGES keeping an eye on all the different dogs in the neighbourhood and one day he notices a shaggy labradoodle walking through town, carrying a newspaper in its mouth. Albie follows the labradoodle and eventually the dog leads Albie Short to a park bench, and on the park bench are a man and a woman. The dog jumps on to the bench and hands over the newspaper, and Albie Short hears the woman say, 'Oh look, dear, there's an article about our latest robbery!' And that's when Albie Short knows he's on to something and that's also when Albie Short takes a photo of them and gives it to the police.

Tom opened up *Gotcha!* and started to read:

The photograph taken by Albie Short turned out to be the vital evidence the police needed. Police used the photograph to track the criminals down to their caravan. The caravan was full of stolen goods and it was also full of dog hair.

'See,' said Tom. 'The dog was the thing to watch, not the robbers themselves.'

I looked at Tom, all wondering, because I didn't want to ask a silly question in case I had got the wrong end of the stick, but then again I couldn't remember the Stonely newspaper article talking about one single dog (which was a shame because I love dogs more than any other animal).

'Do the Stonely Robbers have a dog then?' I asked, looking at the article again.

'No!' said Tom. 'But that's not my point. My point is that the dog is the clue that leads Albie to the robbers.'

'Oh, I see,' I said, even though I didn't have a clue what Tom was talking about.

'What I mean,' said Tom, popping his Albie Short book in the back pocket of his jeans, 'is that we need to focus on the clues because the clues will lead us to the criminals.'

Pip stopped doing a handstand and looked at Tom all sparkly. She picked up the newspaper and read the story in silence. When she had finished reading she looked up at me and Tom and whispered: 'Rucksacks. Red balaclavas. Old sheds.'

'Precisely,' said Tom, grinning at Pip and nodding at me. 'Those are the three clues and we need to look for them.'

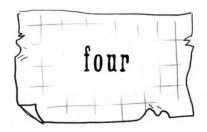

four

Tom said the odds of finding any robbers in Muddlemoor were low to middling and we would probably have to look further afield. But Pip pointed out that in Muddlemoor you never could tell because we've known for ages that it is a hotspot for crime, and Tom nodded because that was quite a good point of Pip's.

I asked Tom if Albie Short ever sat in the park, gathering his thoughts, but Tom said that Albie Short never sits still if he can help it because Albie Short is always on the lookout.

At that point Tom said that he wasn't going to sit around waiting for something to happen because he could give Albie Short a run for his money.

'We need to be proactive,' he said, putting the last Fruit Pastille in his mouth and jumping to his feet. 'We need to search this village from top to bottom. We need to hunt out every nook and cranny until we have a list of suspects.'

I was a bit sad about having to leave the park because sitting under the zip wire, chatting and eating Fruit Pastilles is one of my best things to do in life, but when Tom is being proactive he is quite hard to argue with. Like, for instance, once, when I was staying with Tom and Pip at their house in Wales, Tom decided we should make our own den at the bottom of the garden, and it took us eight hours to make that den and we didn't even stop to watch *Ninja Heroes*.

Tom said we should split up now so we could cover more of the village.

'Remember what we're looking for,' he reminded us. 'Rucksacks, red balaclavas, old sheds. Keep your eyes peeled, keep your wits about you and don't miss a trick.'

I wasn't sure what my wits were but I didn't want to

sound stupid by asking the others so I pressed my lips together and tried really hard not to say one word in case a stupid question popped out, because one thing I can't help doing is asking stupid questions in front of people when I'm not meant to. Like, for instance, once, when my class was learning about the Battle of Trafalgar, Mrs Vukovitch asked if anyone knew why Lord Nelson was on top of Nelson's Column in Trafalgar Square, and I said, 'Is it because he climbed up there with one arm?' because that's what Bella had told

me AS A JOKE, and the whole class burst out laughing, and even Mrs Vukovitch had a coughing fit, and I went bright red because Bella had been teasing me.

'Meet at the top of Church Lane in thirty minutes,' said Tom, heading towards the village hall at top speed.

I put my hand in my pocket and discovered the plastic gold medal I won at school for taking part in the bike agility class. I put my fingers round it and wondered if maybe a plastic gold medal counted as wits and then I kept my eyes peeled for clues.

I really wished we could have stuck together when we were going round the village because I didn't exactly know what I would do if I did discover a true-life criminal gang. I was a bit scared.

I walked up and down through Golders Close and Tiddlington Road, but even though I saw lots of sheds in people's gardens they were mostly really new and I could see people going in and out of them with forks and plant pots. And when the people spotted me staring at them, they waved at me – which guilty criminals

DEFINITELY wouldn't do.

I waved back at a man and a woman in their twenties with matching blond hair. They were painting their shed blue and listening to music. They didn't look like burglars.

I got a bit suspicious when I walked past the Flettons' house in Golders Close because there were a few red things hanging on the washing line and for a split second I wondered if they were maybe balaclavas, but when I got a bit closer I saw that they were matching red jumpers. That made sense because the Fletton twins are two and a half and they are always wearing identical clothes that need washing all the time because they dribble a lot and they are messy eaters.

Nobody I bumped into was wearing a balaclava because it was quite a warm day and I didn't see any rucksacks either, just a couple of shopping trolleys.

Luckily, when I checked my watch, I realised that it was nearly time to meet the others so I headed up Church Lane. The vicar was watering plant pots outside the church. 'Hello, young man,' he said, and I stopped to chat to him about the church roof and other quite boring things. Then the vicar asked me if I was going to come to Stay and Play at the church on Sunday. I didn't say anything because the truthful answer to that was 'No' and I didn't fancy being rude.

Luckily, I spotted Tom walking up Church Lane and behind him, running with her hair flying, was Pip.

'More recruits for Stay and Play on Sunday!' the vicar said, smiling at Tom and Pip and then turning away to carry on with his watering.

But Tom just nodded vaguely because he was really busy looking at the vicar's shed. Tom whispered that maybe the vicar was helping to hide the Stonely Robbers' loot in his shed in exchange for money to mend the church roof.

Tom said he was going to test the vicar's GUILTY REFLEX by casually mentioning the Stonely robberies and watching to see how he (the vicar) reacted. Tom explained that this was one of Albie Short's most effective tricks.

'Have you heard of the Stonely Robbers, vicar?' he asked in a loud voice. We all glued our eyes to the vicar's face.

'I certainly have,' said the vicar, sadly. 'I've been double locking the church every night because things keep going missing. But, then again, I'd lose my head if it wasn't screwed on.'

The vicar looked at us carefully. 'Luckily Muddlemoor is a nice safe place,' he said. 'Nothing for you dear children to worry about.'

None of us said one word because we knew the truth, i.e. that Muddlemoor is one of the most dangerous villages in the whole of the UK. We searched the vicar's face to see if he was going red or biting his nails (because according to Albie Short these are the tell-tale signs of a guilty culprit) but the vicar just started humming.

We took a closer look inside the shed but it was full of forks and spades and old plant pots and definitely wasn't big enough to hide a gang of robbers or their stolen goods.

Plus, the vicar started talking about getting a burglar alarm for the church which is not something he would do or say if he had links to a criminal gang.

'False alarm,' muttered Tom sadly.

We said goodbye to the vicar and headed back down Church Lane.

five

I asked Tom and Pip if they had seen anything suspicious, e.g. an old shed, or someone in a red balaclava with a rucksack out and about in the village, but they shook their heads.

'The Stonely Robbers must be lying low,' said Tom, and Pip kicked a stone into a skip. I told Tom about the red jumpers at the Flettons' house and he shrugged his shoulders and said, 'Red herring,' and when I asked him what 'red herring' meant he said, 'Don't you know?' and forgot to explain.

At the corner near the shop we stopped outside a posh house that is owned by a family who live abroad most of the time. We expected it to be empty like it usually is, but straightaway we saw two children playing in the garden on a swing made from an old tyre, hanging from a big walnut tree. We stopped to watch because it was quite exciting seeing people in this garden and we wanted to know what the new people looked like. The youngest child (a girl of about five) was trying to do a cartwheel but kept falling over. She spotted us and waved.

I waved and said, 'My cousin Pip is AMAZING at gymnastics. She could show you how to do cartwheels.' And then I pointed at Pip.

The girl smiled and ran over to us but Pip didn't smile back. She stared at the ground and said, 'My back hurts, I can't do cartwheels at the moment.'

I suddenly remembered

about Pip not doing gymnastics in front of people because she didn't like the attention. 'Sorry,' I said, 'I forgot.' And Pip shrugged her shoulders and said, 'Don't worry.'

Luckily the children turned out to be REALLY friendly and normal. The eldest, a boy about my age, told us they lived a long way away in Asia most of the time because their parents had jobs in a place called Jakarta. 'We much prefer it in Muddlemoor, though,' he said, 'because it isn't too hot and there aren't any mosquitoes. Also, our uncle lives here and he shows us how to paint pictures.'

'Children!' called a voice. 'Go and get your rucksacks, we're going into Stonely for dinner!'

The children went inside.

'Did you hear what the mum said?' I whispered.

Tom frowned. 'She just asked them to get ready to go into Stonely.'

'Yes,' I said. 'But she also told them to get their RUCKSACKS.'

I suddenly felt really clever and important, a bit like the time Mrs Vukovitch asked me to be Library Monitor and gave me a solid gold badge that said, 'Librarian' in green engraved writing.

Tom and Pip blinked and at first I couldn't tell what they were thinking, but then they looked up and I knew they didn't think I was being silly because they both had glittery stars in the corners of their eyes.

'But if they're rich already,' said Pip, 'why would they need to steal things?'

'Maybe that's WHY they're rich!' I said. 'Maybe it's because they spend their life travelling the world doing robberies.'

I was quite pleased with myself because I am not known for being able to answer questions when I am put on the spot.

Tom chewed his lip. 'But children don't tend to be in gangs of robbers because of having to go to school and do swimming lessons.'

This was true. I looked for signs that the house was

owned by a criminal gang, but the garden was full of toys and a sprinkler and there were old hoodies lying on the ground. It looked like any normal family garden.

'Let's wait and see what the parents look like,' said Tom, and I couldn't argue with this idea because it was sensible.

A long time passed while we waited for the family to come out.

'Maybe they're getting changed into their balaclavas?' I said. 'And getting weapons ready?'

'Or maybe they're putting on coats and trainers and going to the loo like any normal family,' said Tom.

'Is it another red herring?' I asked and Tom shrugged because he doesn't tend to take other people's suspicions as seriously as his own.

Eventually the front door opened and the family started walking down their front path, towards us.

The mum and dad looked really normal, and straightaway I could see that the boy's rucksack was red with green stripes and the girl's was shaped

like a unicorn's head.
Plus they were
ABSOLUTELY TINY.

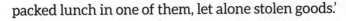

'There's no way
those are getaway
bags,' said Tom.
'You could barely fit a
packed lunch in one of them, let alone stolen goods.'

We waved to the family and they waved back and then we turned to go. Even though I was REALLY disappointed that my idea didn't add up, I was also slightly relieved because I had quite liked the look of that family and I was glad they weren't true-life criminals.

We started walking back to Granny's house. None of us said much but I knew we were all disappointed. We'd spent the whole afternoon looking for clues and had just come to lots of dead ends. It wasn't just that we didn't have enough evidence to link anyone to the crime. It was that, deep down in our hearts, we didn't really believe that the vicar or the nice family were responsible.

'It's all about hunches,' said Tom, taking *Trapped!* (the second Albie Short book) out of his back pocket. 'Listen.'

Albie Short looked at the old woman. He noticed every detail of her appearance, from her pale pink glasses to her green leather handbag with the gold clasp. He took in her neat grey hair and her pearl necklace. Everything about her looked trustworthy and respectable. Except Albie knew deep down in his heart that she was not trustworthy and respectable. Albie had the strangest feeling that everything she did or said was a lie. He had no reason to suspect this woman but he had a hunch and Albie took hunches very seriously. Albie's hunches were usually right.

'Sometimes,' said Tom, 'a hunch is worth more than a notebook full of evidence.'

I looked carefully at Tom.

'Do you have a hunch?' I asked.

'No,' said Tom, closing the book, 'but I'm open to ideas.'

I sighed. We were no closer to finding the Stonely Robbers than we'd been this morning. We trudged on up the main road through the village, back towards Granny's house.

We were nearly at Little Draycott when we were overtaken by Chris Norris on his bike. Even though Chris Norris doesn't say much and smells of cigarettes and damp clothes, we can't help being interested in him because riding a bike with one hand while smoking is impressive behaviour. According to Sophie Pearce, Chris Norris lost his arm when he was a teenager but he has never let it hold him back in life. Sophie Pearce says that sometimes newspaper journalists come to interview him. Once I asked Sophie Pearce if Chris Norris was famous and she said, 'Slightly.'

'All right, kids?' said Chris Norris, and we said 'hello' back and then he biked past us. As soon as he turned the corner, Tom said, 'Did you see that?' in a really urgent voice, and I said, 'What?' and Pip stopped skipping.

'His shirt!' said Tom.

I shook my head because I am not very good at noticing shirts, especially if they aren't football ones.

'Then you must be blind,' said Tom. 'It was splattered with blood.'

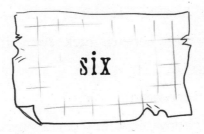

six

The sky was turning dusky and all I wanted to do was run back to Granny's house and curl up with a blanket on her blue velvet armchair. I could see Little Draycott in the distance, all familiar and welcoming. I thought of the oak tree and the tadpole stream and I thought of Granny in her kitchen, listening to the radio and cooking our dinner.

'Are you sure it was blood?' I asked.

'Positive,' said Tom, staring at Chris Norris as he cycled away from us.

Pip went even more thoughtful than usual. 'Where do you think he goes on that bike?' she said, narrowing her eyes.

'The pub?' I suggested.

'Wrong direction,' said Tom.

'Unless he's coming back from the pub and going home.'

'He lives opposite the pub.'

I didn't know how Tom knew this but I wasn't surprised because one thing about Tom is that he usually finds out things before me and Pip.

'Suspicious, isn't it?' said Tom. 'If you think about it.'

I didn't reply because my mind had started to wander and the thing I was thinking about was KitKats and as far as I knew there was nothing suspicious about them.

Tom fished out the folded newspaper article from his back pocket and opened it. He pointed to the bottom paragraph that asked members of the public to keep an eye out for suspicious activities.

'Look,' he said. 'Chris Norris has blood on his shirt and he is always on that bike of his. That's a lot of suspicious activity for one person in a small village. It's pretty obvious to me that Chris Norris has got his hands in something he shouldn't.'

'Hand,' said Pip.

'What?'

'He only has one hand.'

Tom nodded. 'Noted,' he said. 'But what I mean is, it's our civic responsibility to find out what he is up to. Isn't that what the article is telling us to do? Keep an eye out for any suspicious behaviour. What if Chris Norris has something to do with the Stonely robberies? What if we've spent all afternoon looking for clues and now one big clue has just cycled past us? We can't just ignore it. Don't you think we should follow it up?'

I swallowed silently because I was getting hungry and I was quite keen on going back to Granny's house for some food.

'Those were rhetorical questions,' said Tom. 'I'm not expecting either of you to answer.'

Me and Pip looked at each other and Pip gave me a tiny grin.

'The fact is,' said Tom, 'I have a hunch about Chris Norris and remember what Albie Short says about hunches?' He paused. 'Again, rhetorical.'

The sky was now pinkish grey, the same colour as my sister Bella's old rabbit toy that she won't throw away even though she is nearly twenty. It was starting to get dark.

'Oh look, we're at Granny's road,' I said.

But Tom and Pip aren't scared of the dark because they live in the middle of the countryside where there are no street lights. Tom said he wasn't going to leave this stone unturned and, instead of turning right down Little Draycott, he set off along the main road to Stonely behind Chris Norris. Pip went after Tom and I followed them because I didn't fancy getting left behind and having to fib to Granny about what they were up to.

Luckily, Chris Norris was not a very fast biker (probably because of only having one hand) so we managed to catch up with him, but we stayed well back so he wouldn't notice us. Stonely Road was surrounded by high hedges, full of hawthorn and cow parsley and red campion. (The reason we know the names of wild

flowers is because
Granny teaches us when
she takes us for walks.) Tom
told us we had to stay on the right-
hand side of the road so we could
see the cars coming towards
us, but luckily there weren't
any cars coming towards
us because the roads near
Granny's village are very quiet.

Every now and then, Chris
Norris looked back, almost as if
he could sense that somebody
was following him. Whenever
he did this, we hid in the thick
hedge that ran along the
side of the road. Sometimes
we caught our legs and arms
on brambles and nettles.
At one point

we had to stop because Tom slightly cut his knee on a sharp twig and got hysterical because he can't stand the sight of blood, especially when it is his own. While we were waiting for Tom to calm down, Pip pulled a huge bramble thorn out of her arm. She said it didn't hurt, but I knew she was being brave because the thing about Pip is that she is tougher than most people, e.g. Tom.

Once Tom had calmed down and stopped gasping, we ran to catch up with Chris Norris.

'Look!' said Tom. 'He's turning left.'

Chris Norris's bike disappeared through a gap in the hedge. We sprinted along the road until we reached the gap and then we crouched down and peered through. The gap led onto a small field which was divided into little vegetable patches.

'Is it some kind of farm?' asked Tom.

I was quite surprised that Tom thought it was a farm because I knew exactly what it was and I am not used to knowing more than Tom.

'They're allotments,' I said, pointing to the vegetable

patches. 'Where people go to grow their own fruit and veg. Mum's friend Sarah has an allotment next to a railway track. She's always giving us runner beans.'

Pip shuddered because she doesn't eat vegetables if she can help it, especially green ones.

'Ah, allotments,' said Tom, 'I've read about them.'

Chris Norris leaned his bike against a white fence.

'Look,' said Pip, pointing to an old, flaky building the other side of the fence.

And straightaway I started to get all gulpy because it was an old shed.

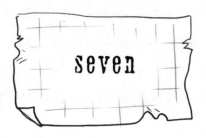

seven

Once when I was much younger, me, Mum and Bella went to a football match at a really big stadium in London. I wandered off because I wanted to look at some football shirts, and then when I tried to find Mum and Bella again I couldn't find them ANYWHERE. Eventually it got really dark and I was completely lost and really frightened, but luckily a policewoman found me and put me on her shoulders and carried me around the football stadium until I spotted Mum and Bella – they had been looking for me in the coffee shop all along. Ever since then I have tried not to get lost in the dark because it is not something I am keen on.

Except now I was out in the nearly dark, a long

way from Granny's, and Tom said we couldn't leave until we'd had a closer look at Chris Norris's shed because we'd spent all day looking for an old shed and we had a duty to investigate what Chris Norris was doing in his.

Tom kept saying, 'Follow the clues, remember,' and grinning. I hopped around from foot to foot because when I am scared of things, e.g. the dark, I mainly get a bit hyper. Pip didn't move a muscle because the dark doesn't frighten her. She is more scared of everyday things such as swimming lessons.

The sky was now the colour of my grey school socks and getting darker every minute. 'Shouldn't we go home while we can still see the road?' I suggested.

'Not until we've seen what he gets up to in that shed of his,' said Tom. 'Let's wait until he comes out.'

Ten minutes went by and the moon started to rise above Chris Norris's shed.

'I'm starving,' I said, trying to sound less scared than I felt.

'Shhhh,' hissed Tom. 'He's coming!'

Chris Norris came out of his shed, whistling. He locked the door behind him and grabbed his bike with his one hand. Then he rode right past us and set off back towards Muddlemoor.

We blinked in the darkening light and looked at each other. Eventually Pip said, 'What would Albie Short do?'

Tom creeped over to the shed, trying to avoid treading on carrots and broad beans. 'Albie Short would evaluate the evidence.'

My heart went all sinky because at that moment in time I didn't want to evaluate evidence. I wanted to get away from this dark allotment and back to Granny's.

Tom tried to open the shed door but it was locked and the windows were too high up to see through.

'I'll keep a lookout,' he said. 'Pip, you climb on Joe's back and peep through the windows.'

I looked over my shoulder, worried that Chris Norris was going to cycle back and catch us looking through his shed window.

'You have better balance than me,' said Tom.

'Do I?' I said, because even though I was thinking about the dark, I couldn't help being pleased that Tom had noticed my good balancing skills. For example, in

PE at school when we have to stand on one leg with our arms in the air, I am always the last one to fall over. If balancing was a job, I could earn quite a lot of money.

I held on to the bottom of the shed windowsill while Pip climbed up my back and onto my shoulders. She stood up slowly.

'What can you see?' said Tom.

I concentrated on not moving a muscle.

'Erm,' said Pip from above.

'What is it?' said Tom. 'Is it red balaclavas??'

My legs started to shake.

'Hang on,' said Pip, leaning towards the window. 'It's really dark in there, I need to get a closer look.'

Pip never blurts things out until she is completely sure. Which is the opposite of some people, e.g. me. Like, for instance, in Pip's school reports her teachers say she should put up her hand more in class and tell everybody what she is thinking. But my teacher, Mrs Vukovitch, says I should STOP putting up my hand and interrupting until I have something important to say.

Pip climbed down from my shoulders and looked at us.

'What's in there?' said Tom.

Pip frowned. 'Well,' she said, 'it's a bit odd. The whole shed is full of . . . paintings.'

'Tins of paint you mean?'

'No. Pictures and drawings – you know, ART.'

I was a bit disappointed about this because for the last few minutes I had been convinced that Chris Norris was definitely involved in the Stonely robberies and I had even pictured me, Tom and Pip on the front page of the local newspaper with a headline, saying 'Local children discover Stonely Robbers' hideout'.

But now it looked like we had come across another red herring – first the vicar, then the family who owned the most expensive house in the village and now Chris Norris.

'Never mind,' I said, turning back towards the main road, 'we can always look for more clues tomorrow.' I got ready to walk back to Granny's.

But Tom let out a HUGE breath. 'What if the Stonely Robbers are also art thieves? What if those paintings are stolen art?'

And that's when I knew we were caught up in something HUGE.

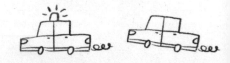

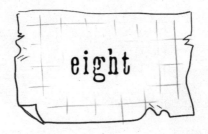

eight

We ran back at top speed because it was getting hard to see anything in front of us. As we turned into Little Draycott we heard Granny calling our names.

'Here we are!' I said, rushing to give her a hug.

'I was about to send out a search party,' said Granny. 'I don't like you being out after dark!' and she gave me a big hug back.

'Dinner's ready,' she continued. 'I'm feeding you before my book club guests arrive. I'm not going to eat because I'm planning to gorge on cheese later.'

While we ate chicken pie and green beans (Pip left the green beans on the corner of her plate under a bit of pastry) we watched Granny arrange cheese and

Black
Bomber
- - - →

biscuits on the table, including a cheese called Black Bomber which doesn't actually look like cheese because it is covered in hard black wax and is really heavy. 'I always think the Black Bomber looks like a lethal weapon,' said Granny, giggling, but we did not giggle back because it was a bit strange to hear your own grandmother talking about a lethal weapon.

After supper, we escaped upstairs because Granny was getting the kitchen ready for her guests and we wanted to discuss Chris Norris, A.K.A. the Art Thief, A.K.A. the Stonely Robber.

'He doesn't LOOK like an evil criminal,' said Pip

because another thing about Pip is that she doesn't like saying bad things about people. 'And he's always been really friendly to us, remember.'

'You can't trust appearances,' said Tom, opening *Trapped!*. 'Listen to this.'

Albie Short looked at his description of Scarlett Peasgood. She had soft brown hair, dimples on her cheeks and caramel freckles all over her nose. When she smiled you couldn't help smiling too because her face was so friendly. She looked like just the sort of person you would want to go camping with. She did not look anything like a spy, but she happened to be the most dangerous spy in Europe.

'When it comes to criminals,' said Tom, 'you never can tell. What we have to do now is track down the remaining four members of the gang. My guess is they're hiding out in Chris Norris's house.'

I looked out of our bedroom window towards The Old Boot pub near where Chris Norris lived. I half expected to see people wearing red balaclavas and carrying rucksacks in the distance, but it was too dark to see anything except the branch of the magnolia tree in Granny's front garden.

'At least we're nice and high up here,' said Tom. 'It means we can keep a lookout for potential robbers without them spotting us first. People always built castles on the tops of hills to protect themselves against enemy invasion.' Tom started talking about a man from history called William the Conqueror who built a lot of castles on hills. I slightly stopped listening at this point because history is not a favourite subject of mine, but then Tom mentioned William the Conqueror's booby traps and I started to concentrate again because one of my main hobbies in life is making booby traps. Once I balanced a Tupperware pot full of water on top of the kitchen door, and when Bella and her friend Rosie opened the door, the water spilled all over them and it was hilarious.

We had a good hunt for things to use for a booby

trap, e.g. a plastic dart and a handful of gravel and a plastic cup filled with water, because even though deep down we knew that we weren't much of a match for a gang of armed robbers, we also knew we couldn't just sit there and do nothing for days on end.

When Granny's book club guests arrived we were a bit temped to test out our booby traps on them, but as soon as we started dripping water out of the window, Bob Merry looked up

and spotted us. He smiled and waved so then we had to go downstairs and say hello.

Granny was all chatty and excited because Thursday evenings are the highlight of her week. Granny says there is only one thing better in life than curling up in an armchair with a really good book – and that is meeting up with her friends to talk about a really good book.

But I don't know why Granny gets so excited about talking about books. Talking about books is not as good as making putty or inventing a new joke or setting off Fun Snaps. Thinking about Fun Snaps reminded me of the box I had at the bottom of my suitcase. I had bought them last week with some of my birthday money and I had completely forgotten to take them out of my bag to show Tom and Pip. But I couldn't tell my cousins about them now because they were too busy being polite to grown-ups and talking to them about books. Talking about books is harder than it sounds.

Even though Tom is a big reader (he even reads on

holiday when he could be jumping off the pier), he doesn't see the point in TALKING about books. Pip is not so much of a reader because she's keener on gymnastics and she only speaks when she has to, e.g. when she wants to go to the toilet in the middle of a maths lesson.

'Hello, rotters!' said Anthea. 'Not planning to spy on us this evening, are you?'

'No!' we said at the same time.

'Oh, what a shame!' said Anthea, nudging Bob Merry. 'I do love a Muddlemoor mystery!' Anthea and Bob laughed really loudly and Mrs Mackintosh (the strict head teacher from the next-door village) snorted like a horse.

We did not laugh because for one thing it wasn't funny and for another thing we weren't even planning to eavesdrop at the door because we were not one bit interested in listening to them argue about books.

'Come and have a glass of wine,' said Granny, leading Anthea, Bob Merry and Mrs Mackintosh into her kitchen.

We escaped into the sitting room so we wouldn't get trapped in any more grown-up conversation, and we switched on *Ninja Heroes* because it is one of our favourite programmes on telly. But it was really hard to hear *Ninja Heroes* because Granny's kitchen is right next to the sitting room, and the walls in her house are very thin, and the people in Granny's book club were speaking in really loud voices, probably because most of them have hearing aids.

Pip and I moved closer to the telly so we could watch a woman called Patti Jay fall into green slime. Next came Roy, a firefighter wearing a Spider-Man suit. He made it all the way to the final wall, but he wasn't strong enough to get to the top. Roy said he was 'gutted' and that he would keep training and come back again next year.

'Strange,' said Tom.

'He's not strange, he just likes being Spider-Man,' I said because I thought Tom was talking about Roy.

'Not HIM,' said Tom. 'In the kitchen! I've been

listening to them. They're not arguing about books, they're not even TALKING about books. And it's meant to be a book club.'

Straightaway, me and Pip stopped watching *Ninja Heroes* and listened. Tom was right. The members of Granny's book club weren't discussing books, they were talking about something completely different, but the only words I could make out properly were 'Saturday' and 'secret' (and they all seemed to be saying 'shhhh').

'Surely the whole point of a book club is to TALK ABOUT BOOKS,' said Tom, crossly.

At that point the doorbell rang. We assumed it was another member of Granny's book club, e.g. Ronnie Mehta, and rushed to answer the door because we like Ronnie Mehta and Granny always lets us answer the door as long as we check who the person is first. But for once Granny got to the door before us.

'Come in, come in!' she said to the person. 'We're all here, discussing books – or not as the case maybe!'

Granny spotted us hovering in the hall outside the sitting room.

'Ooooh,' she said, turning around to face the person at the front door. '*Pas devant les enfants.*'

I looked at my cousins and they looked at me. '*Pas devant les enfants*' means 'Not in front of the children' in French and it is what grown-ups say when they don't want us to hear what they are talking about. But we know what it means because Tom keeps a French dictionary on him at all times and he is practically fluent in French. When grown-ups say, '*Pas devant les enfants*' we always start listening extra carefully because we know they are going to start saying something interesting and unsuitable.

Except I don't think the person at the door was even slightly fluent in French because he said, 'Sorry I'm late' in a really gruff voice.

At first, we couldn't see who he was because Granny was blocking our view, but on their way to the kitchen, he said, 'All right, kids,' and we GASPED because it

wasn't Ronnie Mehta and it wasn't any of Granny's usual friends.

It was Chris Norris.

And he was carrying a massive blue rucksack.

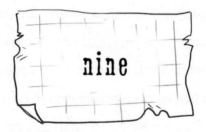

nine

The next morning, Tom said he had been up all night thinking about Chris Norris and reading Albie Short books and coming up with a plan. Staying up all night is not unusual behaviour for Tom because he doesn't need as much sleep as most people. Once, Tom stayed up all night reading four science books and in the morning he had bits of blood in his eyes from reading so much and his mum made him stay off school to sleep it off, except he didn't sleep it off, he started doing science experiments in his bedroom. That's how mad about reading Tom is – and that's also how keen he is on science.

I wasn't surprised that Tom had come up with a plan because he usually tends to be the best at it, especially when we are staying with Granny and ESPECIALLY when it comes to tracking down dangerous criminals.

Mainly when Tom comes up with a plan it involves me and Pip having to do risky and dangerous things. Mum is always saying that I shouldn't do everything Tom tells me to do, but I don't mind doing what Tom says because Tom's plans are normally really exciting.

Tom said that in his opinion Chris Norris was the leader of the Stonely Robbers and it was our responsibility to catch him red-handed, with the rest of the gang, before they carried out another robbery. Tom said Chris Norris was obviously the sort of thief who would steal anything – cash, art, you name it – and that he probably had his eye on Granny's jewellery collection and that's why he had come over last night with his big blue rucksack.

'Was he casing the joint then?' asked Pip, and Tom said, 'In my opinion, yes.' I didn't say anything because I couldn't quite remember what 'casing the joint' meant, but I agreed with Tom and Pip that we had to keep

Chris Norris away from Granny's jewellery.

'I've already checked the laundry basket in the spare room,' said Tom, 'and her jewellery is still there. But there's a strong chance Chris Norris will be back and next time I guarantee he won't be alone.'

Tom said we had to follow Chris Norris for the whole day and find out who his accomplices were. 'Tracking down Chris Norris,' said Tom, 'is a matter of urgency.'

'But what if Chris Norris doesn't meet up with the rest of the gang today?' asked Pip. Pip is good at spotting problems and she is also good at staying calm in a crisis.

'He will,' said Tom, sounding a lot more certain than I was. 'The thing about robbers is they are always planning their next heist. They need a regular fix.'

Tom picked up *Trapped!* and told us there was a

character in the second Albie Short book called Sally Crossing who was so addicted to burglary she had to commit a robbery before breakfast every morning – or she couldn't eat her Bran Flakes.

All through breakfast we started planning how we were going to spend the morning spying on Chris Norris. We decided to go straight to his allotment and hide behind the raspberry cage and wait for him to turn up so we could catch him red-handed with stolen property (and possibly with the rest of the gang). But then Granny ruined everything, she went all fidgety and told us that she needed to go into Stonely to 'run some errands'.

'OOH,' I said all gloopy, because my mouth

was full of cereal. 'If we go into Stonely, can we go to the Birds Nest for a milkshake?' For about twelve seconds I completely forgot about spying on Chris Norris because going to the Birds Nest is one of my favourite things about staying with Granny.

The Birds Nest is in the market hall and it is a really small café that has boxes for chairs. In the Birds Nest the knives and forks are kept in old baked bean tins and there are antique typewriters on the tables that you can play with whenever you want. Uncle Marcus says the place is a 'health hazard' but he is wrong because the Birds Nest is amazing. The chef there makes milkshakes that come in jam jars with red and white stripy straws.

Even though I was really excited about sneaking to Chris Norris's shed and following him and tracking down the rest of the criminal gang, I couldn't help wanting to go to the Birds Nest for a milkshake more because that's how good the Birds Nest milkshakes are.

But Granny shook her head.

'Sorry, you lot,' she said in a faraway voice because

she was concentrating on looking at a list. 'For once I can't take you with me. Anyway, I'm sure you'd just get bored of me dashing around running errands. But don't worry, I've asked Rupi and Nina Mehta to come and babysit you until I come back.'

I almost spat out my cereal. I could not BELIEVE that Granny was going into Stonely WITHOUT US, and I was even more shocked that she was planning to leave us with a babysitter.

One thing me and my cousins don't need is a babysitter. For instance, we know how to put the rubbish in the recycling bin, and we understand not to answer the door without checking who is ringing the bell, and we are one hundred per cent up to speed with Granny's dishwasher. The main thing about us is that we are fine on our own.

Tom says we could survive without grown-ups on a desert island and I agree with him because, once, Granny let us watch a film called *Castaway* about a man who lives on a desert island and survives by catching fish and eating coconuts and making friends with a basketball called Wilson.

Tom said talking to a basketball was the first sign of madness but Pip said it was a form of survival. Tom and Pip had a bit of an argument about this and Tom asked me which of them was right, but I didn't answer because I wasn't sure.

Tom cleared his throat.

'We'll come and help you, Granny,' he said. 'We love running errands.'

This wasn't strictly true or accurate, but what Tom meant is that running errands is way better than being stuck at home with Rupi and Nina Mehta who probably wouldn't even let us outside on our own. And if we couldn't go out to keep an eye on Chris Norris and his shed, we'd rather be in Stonely with Granny.

'Thank you, Tom, but I'll be absolutely fine on my own,' said Granny. And then she laughed and wouldn't look us in the eye. This made me go a bit flibberty because I know for a fact that when someone won't

look you in the eye it is a SIGN THEY MIGHT BE HIDING SOMETHING. The reason I am one hundred per cent sure about this is because, once, a real-life detective inspector came in to our school to talk about his job and he told us that one of the good ways to tell if a suspect is hiding something is if they refuse to look him in the eye.

I really wanted to tell Tom and Pip about the not-looking-at-us-in-the-eye guilt thing, but Granny kept putting away cereal boxes and wiping the table so I had to be patient even though patience doesn't come naturally to me.

Eventually, Granny went to get her handbag from upstairs and I tried to tell the others about Granny not looking at us in the eye but before I could get my words out, Tom started talking.

'Babysitters are a real problem for us,' he said crossly. 'We are not babies and we need to be able to go out to hunt down robbers.'

We cleared up our cereal bowls because that is

something we always have to do when we're staying at Granny's, but while we were loading the dishwasher Pip said, 'I'm a bit worried about Granny going into Stonely without us because what about all the armed robbers on the loose?'

I stopped loading the dishwasher and Tom said, 'That's why it's paramount that we find out what Chris Norris is up to.' (Tom is always using long words, e.g. paramount.)

I carried on stacking the dishwasher in silence because the idea of Granny being in danger was actually REALLY SCARY. I waited for Tom to come up with a new plan of action, but before he could say anything Granny came back downstairs and grabbed her coat.

'Right,' she said. 'I wonder where those Mehta girls are.'

Tom tried telling Granny again that she didn't need to ask Rupi and Nina to babysit us because we were mature and responsible enough to look after ourselves, but Granny laughed and did up her buttons.

After that there wasn't any more time to persuade her to cancel her trip into Stonely because the doorbell rang and it was Rupi and Nina Mehta on their bikes and, about a millisecond after they wheeled their bikes into the hall, Granny said 'Cheerio,' and 'Be good!' and then she whizzed out to her car. She barely even waved.

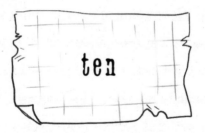

ten

Rupi and Nina had loads of revision to do so they spread their school books all over the kitchen table as if it was THEIR kitchen. Even though we definitely didn't need looking after, we couldn't help thinking that Rupi and Nina should have been doing SOMETHING to entertain us seeing as Granny was paying them. Like, for instance, they could have baked a cake or played Monopoly, or at least pretended to protect us from the gang of robbers on the loose. But Rupi and Nina didn't notice our cross faces. All they did was talk about how much money they still needed to earn for a school trip to Rwanda over the summer. 'We're still £750 short,' said Rupi, jotting down numbers on a scrap piece of paper. 'That's a lot of babysitting. We're going to have to think of new ways to make money. I'm going to ask about getting a job in The Old Boot, washing up.'

Nina nodded and said, 'Mrs Rooney has given me a paper round, and Sophie Pearce says we can help with the chickens when she is away, and Dad says he'll pay us to cook and clean if we do it properly. Also, Emma Fletton says she might need some help with her twins because she's going to start working part time from home.'

It was quite boring listening to Rupi and Nina discuss ways to make money and eventually we asked if we could go out for a walk around the village. 'Granny always lets us,' I said helpfully. Nina shrugged her shoulders and said, 'Sure, whatever,' but Rupi nudged Nina and shook her head and then they changed their minds and told us we could only go in the garden. 'We need to keep an eye on you,' said Rupi.

This was REALLY ANNOYING because for one thing Granny always lets us go out into the village on our own and for another thing, finding out what Chris Norris was up to was a matter of criminal importance.

I reminded Rupi and Nina that we are mature and sensible children and we would never do anything silly, e.g. crack our heads open on the zip wire or step into the road without checking.

'That's weird,' said Rupi, grinning, 'because before we came over, Dad told us that you kids get yourselves into trouble the moment the grown-ups' backs are turned. Dad told us to keep a close eye on you.'

'Stay in the garden, buddies,' said Nina, picking up a history book.

So we went outside to play football but then Pip scored an amazing goal against Tom and Tom's foot started to hurt so we stopped for a rest.

'Hello, you three!' said a voice from the next-door garden and it was Sally Merry who was training her dog Puff to sit. The Merrys got Puff last December. According to Granny, Sally loves Puff more than life itself. Even though Puff is still only a puppy she is already massive because she is a giant poodle. Sally takes Puff to puppy classes in the village hall every Thursday evening (which is why she doesn't come to book club with Bob), but Puff is still really naughty.

Puff jumped over the wall into Granny's garden so we played with her for a bit. Tom tried to show her how to fetch a ball but Puff ignored Tom and took the ball back to Sally. Then she jumped back over the wall and ran around the garden in circles, barking.

Sally told us that she was feeling VERY old because she was going to be seventy on Saturday. 'Look at my wrinkles,' she said, pointing to her forehead and even though her wrinkles looked exactly like crinkled paper I didn't say this out loud because it might have hurt her feelings.

Puff barked. 'See!' said Sally, smiling. 'Even Puff agrees about my wrinkles!'

I asked where Bob was and Sally explained that

he had gone into Stonely to run some errands. Then she told us she had some fig rolls in the kitchen and she went inside to get them.

When Sally came back she gave us a packet of fig rolls and told us that we were growing up too fast (which is something grown-ups are always saying to me even though I'm one of the slowest growers in Year 4). We smiled at Sally and stroked Puff and then it started to rain so we took the fig rolls back to Granny's instead of going to our usual hiding place under the weeping willow tree in Ronnie Mehta's garden.

The problem was, we had forgotten that Rupi and Nina were in the kitchen (they had stopped revising now and were watching videos on their phones).

'Back already?' said Rupi, as if we were interrupting her.

Tom offered them a fig roll because offering people food before eating it yourself is one of Granny's rules.

 Rupi took three fig rolls and handed the packet to Nina.

'Thanks,' said Nina, grabbing two fig rolls and putting the half-eaten pack down on the table in front of her.

We stomped upstairs. We couldn't believe what was happening right in front of our eyes. Not only were our babysitters ignoring us, but they were also trying to starve us. 'Food depravation is dangerous for me,' said Tom. 'I have an unusually fast metabolism and my brain can't function if I don't eat regularly.' Then Tom reminded us about the time he forgot to have breakfast and was sick in his lesson. And even though everybody in his class said it was because he was squeamish about cutting open a pig's heart, Tom knew it was because of his fast metabolism.

'Maybe we should sneak out to Mrs Rooney's to buy some more biscuits?' I said, because right now we needed Tom's brain to function because he was the best at coming up with ideas and there was a dangerous robber – A.K.A. Chris Norris – on the loose in Muddlemoor.

Tom agreed that this was a sensible idea and he also said that sneaking out to the shop was not the same as walking round the whole village so we weren't necessarily ignoring Rupi and Nina – even though we sort of were. Plus, we didn't fancy asking Rupi and Nina's permission because the problem with asking permission is that people usually say no – especially if they are babysitting you for the first time.

Tom got out his wallet and we started discussing the price of biscuits, which is one of our favourite topics of conversation. Between us we had £2.72, which was enough for a packet of fig rolls, even in Mrs Rooney's shop, and it was maybe even enough for Jammy Dodgers or Jaffa Cakes. We crept down the stairs through the hall, past the kitchen, and out of the front door.

It was a sunny day but the village was unusually quiet because lots of people were away on holiday. There was no one in the park or on the tennis court. The Gravels (which is the dark, overgrown shortcut leading from the main road all the way to the shop) looked creepier than ever. Even though we were about to die of starvation we didn't take the shortcut because we never go down The Gravels if we can help it, only in true-life emergencies.

We ran all the way to the shop because Tom doesn't see the point in walking,

especially when we are hungry for biscuits. In Wales where they live, Tom and Pip go to a running club every Monday evening and sometimes they run up and down steep hills FOR FUN. This is why it's hard for me to keep up with them and it's also why they don't get stitches in their stomachs like I do.

Anthea was coming out of the shop when we arrived. She waved at us and leaped into her shiny red Mini.

'Can't stop to chat,' she said through her open window. 'I'm late for Janet – Mrs Mackintosh to you lot.

I'm picking her up and then we have to go into Stonely to run some errands.'

Anthea drove off at top speed, TOTALLY ignoring the thirty miles-per-hour signs.

'Hmmmm,' said Tom. 'That's four people running errands in Stonely this morning.'

I didn't say anything because I was mainly thinking about biscuits.

'Granny leaves us with a babysitter for the first time ever because she has to run errands in Stonely,' said Tom. 'Bob Merry leaves Sally to run errands in Stonely. And Anthea breaks the speed limit because . . .'

'She has to run errands in Stonely,' finished Pip. 'With Janet. A.K.A. Mrs Mackintosh.'

'Exactly!' Tom raised his eyebrows. 'Either this is one big coincidence,' he said, 'or they are all in Stonely running errands together.'

Straightaway Pip went all still and staring and then she turned a few cartwheels (because cartwheels sometimes help her think) but then she spotted some people in the distance and stopped doing cartwheels because of not liking people watching her.

'I don't think it's a coincidence,' Pip said, all whispery. 'I think there is a reason.'

(Pip is good at spotting connections and patterns, even when they aren't obvious to anybody else).

'All those people are in Granny's book club,' she said slowly. 'And last night they were talking about something TOP SECRET happening in Stonely on Saturday.'

At this point I went to sit down on a nearby bench because standing up is tricky when you are trying to think and thinking is not always a natural occurrence for me. Tom and Pip sat down next to me.

'Pip's right,' said Tom, frowning. 'But what would they be up to that they wouldn't want anybody to know about?'

We all had a bit of a think about this because it was hard to imagine anything top secret that Granny and her friends might be up to in Stonely. I was just about to tell Tom that I couldn't think of anything when I remembered about Chris Norris joining Granny's book club.

I thought a bit more and then I slowly put my hand up because Tom was acting a bit like a teacher and at my school you aren't allowed to shout out without putting up your hand, even though Dylan Moynihan always does.

I felt more nervous than the time I had to confess to Mrs Vukovitch that I had accidentally worn my alien slippers to school instead of school shoes and couldn't do PE. My mouth felt dry and my heart started doing backflips.

Finally Tom spotted that I had my hand up. 'Yes?' he said.

'What if Granny's book club is a cover up?' I said. 'What if the people in Granny's book club are actually the Stonely Robbers?'

Tom and Pip stared at me for a long time. Pip kept opening her mouth to speak but no words came out because it was probably the most shocking thing I had ever thought, let alone said, in my whole life.

It was so shocking that we turned and walked straight back to Granny's. Pip stayed in the garden for a bit because she wanted to practise her one-handed cartwheel but me and Tom had to go inside and help Rupi and Nina find everything for lunch. It wasn't until later that I realised we had completely forgotten to buy any biscuits.

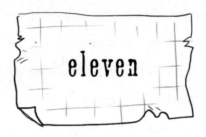

eleven

Even though Nina and Rupi Mehta were not very good at babysitting, and even though at lunchtime they burnt our pizza and forgot to cut up carrot and cucumber for vitamins, and EVEN THOUGH THEY ATE ALL OUR FIG ROLLS, in the end we didn't actually MIND being looked after by them because a) they hadn't noticed that we had sneaked out to go to the shop and b) during lunch they told us stories about a really naughty girl at their school who was always pranking their French teacher and setting off the fire alarm. They also told us what they thought of all the people we knew in Muddlemoor.

'Your gran's all right,' said Nina, 'and I don't mind Bob and Sally when they're not talking about that bonkers puppy of theirs but Anthea can get a life. She keeps asking what subjects we're planning to take for A levels and what university we want to go to. When I told her I wanted to take a gap year, she told me not to be a slacker.'

'She likes improving our education too,' I told them because the thing about being a chatterbox is you can't actually help chatting. 'She says there are a lot of gaps in my brain that need filling.'

Rupi and Nina giggled and this made me keep talking because when I make people giggle I can't help getting a bit carried away.

Another reason I enjoyed chatting to Rupi and Nina was because I was secretly hoping that Tom and Pip might forget about my recent suspicions. I already regretted suggesting that Granny's book club were the Stonely Robbers. I didn't want Granny to be a thief or go to prison because if she went to prison we wouldn't be able to stay with her any more and staying with Granny was probably the best thing

in my whole entire life.

I started telling Rupi and Nina about Dylan Moynihan, but eventually Tom kicked me hard under the table and that's when I realised that he hadn't forgotten about the Granny situation ONE TINY BIT.

So I stopped talking and put my plate in the dishwasher. Then, when Rupi and Nina went back to their revision, me, Tom and Pip raced upstairs to our room.

'Joe Robinson,' said Tom. 'You have made a serious accusation. If what you say is true then we have to stop Granny before she commits her next crime because we can't risk her getting caught by the police because if she gets caught she might end up in prison for the rest of her life.'

Pip slightly yelped and I knew that she was even more worried about Granny going to prison than I was because Pip is allergic to things like holiday clubs and tennis camps.

'But we can't jump to conclusions,' said Tom,

opening up *Trapped!*. 'That's what Albie Short's Uncle Max always says and Albie Short's Uncle Max is an undercover agent.'

Tom turned to a page in the middle of the book and started to read.

Uncle Max looked down at Albie Short from his great height. 'I have three bits of advice to give you before I head back undercover,' said Uncle Max. 'Think before you speak, plan your next move and don't jump the gun.'

Uncle Max stepped inside a car with tinted windows and gave Albie a brief wave. 'Good luck, kiddo,' he said.

'So,' said Tom. 'What are our reasons for suspecting Granny?'

I took a deep breath. 'Well,' I said. 'Granny's book club didn't talk about books AT ALL. They kept whispering and giggling and mentioning something top secret that is happening on Saturday – A.K.A. TOMORROW.'

'Exactly,' said Tom, writing this down in the new notebook that his dad gave him for doing literacy and maths in during the holidays.

'And then,' said Pip, 'in the middle of their book group, Chris Norris turned up with a big rucksack and one of the things the newspaper said was that the Stonely Robbers carried large rucksacks. Also, Chris Norris isn't NORMALLY in their book club AND, EVEN MORE UN-NORMALLY, Chris Norris is hiding stolen property, including paintings, in his shed.'

'The word is abnormally, not un-normally,' said Tom, writing furiously. 'But apart from that, good. Very good.'

Pip did a headstand.

'And, this morning,' I said, all spluttery, 'Granny leaves us with babysitters so she can run errands (which she NEVER normally does) and THEN we find out that the rest of her book club are also in Stonely and they are ALSO running errands.'

'Exactly,' said Tom, sighing. 'Granny hasn't even tried to cover her tracks. My guess is, they're all in it together and they're planning their next heist, tomorrow. I wouldn't be surprised if Chris Norris is in Stonely today too.'

We looked at each other, all gulpy. This was a new situation for us. Normally we are up to our eyeballs PROTECTING Granny from criminals but we had never suspected Granny of being a criminal herself.

We were in shock.

'But why?' I said, all croaky because my voice always goes croaky when I am scared to death. 'Why would Granny and her friends (and Chris Norris) NEED to steal things?'

'I wondered that too at first,' said Tom, 'but it actually makes perfect sense. Granny and her friends are always going on about how expensive everything is, aren't they?'

Me and Pip nodded because this was a true fact.

'And Granny is always telling us to turn off lights

and save paper and not waste money. And also, she likes mending and knitting things rather than buying new stuff BECAUSE IT'S CHEAPER.' I nodded again because Granny is mad about knitting and always sewing on buttons and putting patches on the knees of our jeans. And then I thought of Chris Norris who always wore really old clothes covered in rips and dirt and I suddenly could see why he might need spare cash to buy some new things.

'Plus,' said Tom, 'most old people don't have jobs so they can't earn money of their own.'

'I've thought of something else too,' said Pip, who was still upside down. 'The vicar keeps on asking them for money for the church roof and they can't tell him to go away because that's quite rude and also the thing about vicars is they never give up. That's what Dad says. Maybe Granny and her friends NEED money so they can pay the vicar and make him go away.'

'Yes,' said Tom. 'I think Granny and her book club (plus Chris Norris) have become robbers out of desperation.'

Straightaway I knew that Tom was right because every single word of it made sense.

'But what we don't have,' said Tom, chewing his lip, 'is any hard and fast evidence that the people who were in this house last night – A.K.A. Granny's book club – are a criminal gang.'

'Except for this,' said Pip in a quiet voice.

Me and Tom looked at the medium-sized box in Pip's hands. It was metal and it was locked and I could straightaway tell it was full of money because when she shook it, it made a loud jangling sound.

'I found it next to Granny's magnolia tree when I was practising one-handed cartwheels in the garden earlier,' said Pip. 'I think it's their stash.'

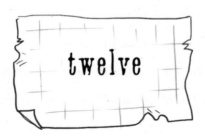

twelve

We sat in our bedroom staring at the cash box. It was locked so we couldn't open it to count how much money was in there, but we knew it was a lot because it was

REALLY heavy.

Tom told us not to touch it with our bare hands because the police would want to check it for fingerprints. He hid it carefully under a blanket in the corner of our room and sat back down.

I waited for a bit because I thought Tom was going to come up with another plan, but he didn't so I started talking.

'Are we going to tell the police?' I asked nervously.

'No,' said Tom. 'The last thing we want is Granny in prison. If she's locked up we won't be able to come and stay with her anymore. We have to do the exact opposite. We have to make sure that Granny DOESN'T get arrested. In other words we need to make sure that her book club doesn't commit any more crimes and if they DO commit a crime, we have to make sure that they don't get caught. EVER.'

I let out a huge, deep sigh because this was a MASSIVE relief but then straightaway I held my breath

again because I wasn't sure how we were going to stop Granny's book club committing their next crime when we didn't even know what or where or when their next crime was.

Tom agreed that we didn't know exactly what their next crime would be or where they would commit it. 'But,' he said, 'I'm working on the assumption that they are planning something for tomorrow.'

I happened to know that assumption means 'something you accept is true without question or proof' because once our head teacher did an assembly about making assumptions and for once I listened to the assembly rather than chatting to Harry O'Kennedy. I was actually a bit surprised to hear Tom making assumptions because mainly Tom is mad about evidence and proof, but when I mentioned this Tom ignored me.

There was a long silence.

'In other words,' Tom said, 'we have to stop them before it's too late.'

'But how?' I asked because I didn't have a clue how we were going to do that.

'I'm not sure,' said Tom, blinking.

For a few minutes we sat there staring at each other, not speaking. I was desperately trying to think of a way to stop Granny and her book club committing their next robbery, but I kept picturing them wearing red balaclavas (because that's what the newspaper article said they wore) and then I got a bit giggly, which sometimes happens to me when I am nervous and excited.

'What's so funny?' asked Tom.

I explained about the red balaclavas but Tom didn't get giggly because he said this was a SERIOUS and DANGEROUS situation. Even though I knew Tom was right I couldn't stop giggling because the thing about giggling is that it is sometimes hard to stop, especially when you know you shouldn't be doing it. Like, for instance, once, when Mrs Vukovitch had yoghurt on her nose, I got really bad giggles and the more she told me to stop the more I couldn't and then I got the hysterics and Mrs Vukovitch sent me to our head teacher's office to calm down.

Pip grinned at me and I started coughing to disguise my giggles, but luckily Tom had stopped looking at me because he had picked up *Target!*, the third Albie Short book, and was reading it at top speed.

After a few minutes he looked up, all sparkly eyed, and I stopped giggling about Granny's book club wearing balaclavas because I could tell that Tom had an idea.

'That's it!' said Tom. 'You've found the solution.'

I said, 'Have I?' because I hadn't actually done anything apart from giggle.

'Yes,' said Tom. 'You remembered about the balaclavas! What we have to do is find Granny's red balaclava and hide it. If she doesn't have a balaclava she won't be able to take part in the robbery tomorrow. Right?'

Me and Pip looked at Tom, all flibberty because it

was a good idea.

'But we don't know where she keeps her balaclava,' I said.

'I know THAT,' said Tom, 'but while she's in Stonely "running errands" we have the perfect opportunity to search this house from top to bottom to find it.'

Rupi and Nina were still in the kitchen so we started at the top of the house. At first everything looked the same as it always did but after a while I started to notice that things didn't feel quite right. Like, for instance, in Granny's bedside cupboard was a really sharp pen knife and anyone could tell that it was not the sort of thing a normal Granny would have next to her bed.

'Is that one of the weapons Granny and the gang use when they commit their robberies?' I asked.

'Yes,' said Tom and shook his head sadly.

In Granny's wardrobe, amongst all the silk scarfs and cardigans, I found a stripy top and it was JUST the sort of the stripy top a burglar wears.

Tom explained that only burglars in films and picture books wear stripy tops, but then Pip said that she had never EVER seen Granny wearing that top, not even once, and that meant it was probably her robbery top

and Tom told me to confiscate the stripy top just in case.

We searched the bathroom and the sitting room and the cupboard under the stairs and we even searched the downstairs loo, but we couldn't find any evidence of a red balaclava. Tom said that Granny was obviously trying to hide evidence that she was one of the Stonely Robbers and maybe she didn't actually hide her balaclava in the house. He said that maybe the whole book club/robbers were hiding their balaclavas in Chris Norris's shed. At this point I felt a bit worried because I really didn't fancy sneaking back to Chris Norris's shed at that moment in time, but then Pip reminded us that we hadn't searched Granny's kitchen yet so we decided to do that first.

'Hi, guys,' said Rupi. 'Do you want anything? Toast? Milk? Juice?'

Me and Pip shook our heads because we didn't think we had time to stop for an afternoon snack but Tom said, 'Yes please,' and winked at us and that's when I realised he was trying to get Rupi and Nina to turn their backs on us so we could search the kitchen.

We pretended we were looking for plates and clean glasses but in actual fact we were searching for evidence of Granny's balaclava. But then Rupi brought over toast and milk so we had to stop looking and sit down at the table. Nina started asking me questions, e.g. how much is a tube ticket in London? And all about the London Dungeons, and I had to answer them, partly because it's rude not to answer when a babysitter asks you a question but mainly because talking about the London Dungeons is one of my favourite topics of conversation.

For a few minutes I slightly forgot about searching for Granny's balaclava because I was busy telling Rupi and Nina all about the stretching machine at the London Dungeons that was used for torturing criminals when Elizabeth I was the Queen of England.

But just when I started telling them about the rats running all over the dungeon floors (and I didn't explain about the rats being pretend because it's a better story if you tell people the rats are real) I spotted Pip's face from the other side of the table and straightaway her face made me stop talking about pretend rats. Pip's cheeks had turned pink and her eyes were HUGE and I knew this wasn't anything to do with my story about the rats and torture machines because Pip had heard my stories loads of times before and was used to them.

Pip pointed at the blue checked armchair in the corner of the kitchen and rolled her eyes back in her head which is what she always does when something shocks her. I turned to look more closely at the chair and straightaway I knew that Pip wasn't looking at the chair itself. She was looking at the thing lying on top of it.

Granny's knitting bag.

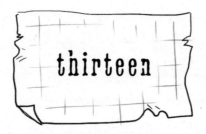

thirteen

I spluttered so loudly that Rupi Mehta thought I was choking on my toast. She got up to get me a glass of water and stood next to me until I'd drunk a few sips. 'Don't go scaring us like that, mate,' she said, patting me on the back and looking a bit worried. So I made myself drink the whole glass of water, even though it was slightly warm and tasted of tap.

When I had finished drinking, I had another look at Granny's knitting bag. This time I didn't even gasp because Tom and Pip were kicking me in the ankle, but I felt like spluttering all over again because there was some knitting sticking out of Granny's knitting bag and it was red.

Tom waited until Rupi and Nina were looking down at their books again and then he leaped up and grabbed the knitting bag and raced out of the room.

'Thanks for the toast,' he called over his shoulder, and beckoned to me and Pip to follow him.

In our bedroom, he unfolded the newspaper article which he was using as a bookmark and keeping in *Target!*. The article was really crumpled now and the newsprint was a bit smudgy but Tom could still read what it said and he read out the bit about balaclavas.

Ms Mason told police that there were five gang members and they were all wearing red balaclavas.

'How many people were there at Granny's book club?' asked Tom.

'Four,' I said.

'Five including Chris Norris,' said Pip.

'Exactly,' said Tom. 'Five. Wearing RED balaclavas.'

He opened up the knitting bag. There were knitting needles still attached to the knitting so we had to hold it very carefully, but as soon as we took it out of the bag we KNEW it was a balaclava because it was a tube shape and it had two holes at one end.

'Eye holes,' said Tom and we nodded because Tom was right.

'Yoo hoo!' came a voice from the bottom of the stairs.

'I'm back!'

We all went gaspy and Pip hid the knitting bag under the bed with Granny's stripy top and the box of money. Then we went to say hello to Granny and we also tried to pretend that we hadn't just discovered the truth, i.e. that she and her book club were the Stonely Robbers.

'Goodness,' said Granny. 'You three look very hot and bothered.'

Tom looked out of the window and said, 'Lovely sunny day!' because his dad, Uncle Marcus, once told him that in the UK people always talk about the weather if they don't know what to say or want to change the subject.

I gave Granny a hug so she wouldn't notice my guilty conscience.

'Did you get your errands done?' said Tom, helping Granny lift a bag onto the table.

'Nearly!' said Granny and then she turned to Rupi and Nina and asked them if we had behaved ourselves.

'No trouble at all,' said Nina.

'Goodness!' said Granny, laughing. 'Are you sure? Well in that case the Terrible Trio deserve these treats from the Birds Nest.'

She handed us a box of brownies, flapjacks, doughnuts and iced biscuits and then she got out her purse and gave Rupi and Nina fifteen pounds each.

'Granny,' I whispered, 'that's a lot of money. Are you sure you can afford that?'

'Oh, don't worry about me,' said Granny. 'I've got plenty of money!'

I felt something cold, a bit like melted ice lolly, run down my throat and into my belly.

'Granny,' I said. My voice sounded all croaky. 'Have you had a sudden windfall?'

Granny burst out laughing and then she put the kettle on and started unpacking the rest of the shopping. I could tell she was avoiding my question because she started asking Rupi and Nina about their exams next term, and Rupi and Nina told Granny all about how they were saving up for a trip to Rwanda in the summer and then Granny handed them ANOTHER ten pounds to 'go towards their Rwanda fund.'

'See,' whispered Tom, 'she's rolling in cash. She's throwing it around,' and me and Pip nodded.

A bit later, when Rupi and Nina had gone home, the phone rang. Granny picked it up and said, 'Oh hello, Bob, long time no see,' and laughed.

We stopped eating the Birds Nest cakes and biscuits so we could listen properly.

'Do you think we'll get away with it?' said Granny, lowering her voice.

We couldn't believe that Granny was discussing her next heist in front of us, in broad daylight.

'Thank heavens,' said Granny. She stopped talking and listened for a minute or two.

We held our breath.

'Yes, twelve p.m. at the Old Bank,' said Granny, all chirpy. 'I'll bring the Black Bomber. We'll see you inside!'

Granny put down the phone and smiled at us.

'I love it when a plan comes together,' she said, picking up her cup of tea.

I looked carefully at Granny's face to see if she was a different person from the one I thought I knew.

'Did you hear what she said?' hissed Tom. 'They're meeting outside the bank. They're planning a bank heist!'

Granny smiled at us but we couldn't smile back because Granny had just admitted over the phone that her book club was planning a BANK HEIST at twelve p.m. in Stonely tomorrow.

'What are you lot whispering about?' she said, nibbling a chocolate brownie.

'Nothing!' we said.

When Granny got up to make herself another cup of tea, Tom said it was too late to try to stop her being a criminal because old people are really set in their ways.

'She's obviously enjoying her new-found wealth,' said Tom. 'This is what happens to people when they get a taste of the high life. They just want more and more. No wonder their next job is a bank.'

I grabbed another piece of cake because when it comes to cake I'm a bit like Granny and I just want more and more.

Tom said that even if we couldn't stop Granny being a bank robber we could TRY to stop her getting arrested and put in prison. He said the first thing to do was move Granny's red knitted balaclava and her stripy top and box of stolen money to a safer hiding place because then if the police came looking for evidence in Granny's house they wouldn't be able to find anything.

Tom also said that although Granny hadn't noticed they were missing yet, we knew it was only a matter of time before she did and then she would search the house from top to bottom until she found them and then WE'D

be in big trouble. We sneaked to our bedroom. Tom put the knitting bag and stripy top under his jumper, I put a blanket over the box of money, and Pip went downstairs to check that Granny wasn't looking. And then we tiptoed through the hall, into the kitchen and out through the French doors into the back garden. We climbed over the walls until we got to Ronnie Mehta's garden and then we hid everything under the blanket, inside the weeping willow tree. And we knew that NOBODY would find it, including the police, because a weeping willow tree is not the sort of place you would ever expect to find accessories to a bank robbery.

As soon as we had hidden the loot, we burst out of the weeping willow tree but straightaway I shrieked really loudly because Rupi and Nina Mehta were sitting on their patio, drinking cups of coffee and staring RIGHT AT US.

We were IN SHOCK because for one thing Rupi and Nina NEVER go into their garden if they can help it and for another thing we didn't know that

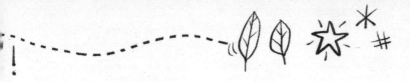

teenagers drank coffee.

'Hi, guys,' said Rupi, waving at us. 'What do you get up to in that tree?'

'Nothing!' I said, because I didn't want to draw their attention to our hiding spot. 'We were just chatting.'

Rupi and Nina laughed and sipped their coffee and then they looked at their phones. 'Bye then!' I said, as breezily as I could manage, and we ran straight back to Granny's to see what was for dinner.

In bed that night we were quieter than usual because, even though we were glad we had managed to hide the box of money and the balaclava and the stripy top, we were now a bit worried that Granny might still try to rob the bank in Stonely tomorrow at twelve p.m. WITHOUT her balaclava. If this happened then everybody, including the police, would be able to see her face when she robbed the bank.

Tom, who was reading *Target!*, said the only thing for it was to ensure that the police didn't lay eyes on

Granny in the first place.

'But how do we do that?' I whispered, and Tom said he wasn't quite sure.

We lay in silence for a bit and I kept trying to think of ways to make sure the police wouldn't see Granny robbing the bank, but then I started to fall asleep because sometimes thinking really hard can make me sleepy.

My eyes were completely closed and I was all drifty when Pip said, 'We need to create a diversion so the police have to investigate another incident when Granny and her book club are robbing the bank.'

'Good idea,' said Tom, and then he and Pip started discussing suitable diversions that might work, but the only things they could think of involved committing a crime ourselves, e.g. breaking into a car or stealing somebody's handbag and this felt too risky and also not very nice.

Tom yawned. 'We'll think of something in the morning,' he said sleepily (because remember he hadn't slept a wink the night before) and then he fell asleep.

But I didn't go to sleep because I started to think of an idea which made me feel really excited and a teeny bit scared.

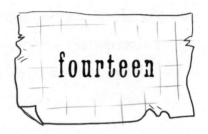

fourteen

Mainly, Granny never tells us what to wear. Like, for instance, she doesn't mind if I wear pyjama bottoms instead of trousers because according to Granny there are more important things to worry about than clothes, e.g. remembering to fill up the bird feeder (our Granny is mad about birds).

But on Saturday morning Granny told us to put on nice shirts and jumpers. 'No tracksuit bottoms with holes in the knees and definitely no pyjamas,' she said, looking at what we were wearing and shaking her head in a pretend cross way.

We stomped up to our room to get changed and Tom said that the reason Granny was behaving strangely was because she was nervous about the prospect of committing a bank robbery in broad daylight. Tom said that it was normal for robbers to get nervous (even if they were really used to committing robberies) and the reason he knew this is because in *Gotcha!* (the first Albie Short book) there was a bank robber who was so nervous he had to stop to go to the toilet whenever he was committing a crime. Tom picked up *Gotcha!* and started reading:

The police caught the robber on his way out of the toilet and when one of the policemen asked the robber if he had washed his hands, the robber started sobbing and said, 'I forgot, guv,' and then he confessed everything to the police and was arrested on the spot in front of a long queue of customers.

Pip and I listened to Tom while we got changed into our worst clothes, e.g. jeans and a woolly jumper for me and dungarees for Pip (which she hates because they have a huge baggy pocket across the tummy and

she can't do gymnastics properly in them). After he'd finished reading, Tom put *Gotcha!* on his bedside table and got dressed in cords and a shirt with buttons and a collar. We all felt cross and itchy and uncomfortable.

'Oh you DO look smart!' said Granny when she saw us. 'Something really important is happening in Stonely today. I can't give the game away at the moment but please don't forget to brush your hair and wipe your faces!'

Granny paused and said, 'I don't suppose any of you have seen my new stripy top? I bought it specially for today.' Me and Pip glanced at Tom and then we all raced back upstairs to brush our teeth because we didn't want to look guilty and give the game away.

'Oh well,' muttered Granny, coming up the stairs behind us. 'I'll just have to wear my old silk blouse instead.'

Tom told us we had to keep track of everything Granny said and did because she was the NUMBER ONE SUSPECT and it was up to us to stop the police arresting her. And then Tom read us another Albie Short paragraph, this time from *Target!*:

Albie Short kept track of everything. He made a note of what people were wearing and how many phone calls they made and what they said and who they said it to. Albie Short missed nothing.

After that we were so busy trying to be like Albie Short that I completely forgot to tell Tom and Pip about the idea I had thought of last night when they were asleep. All morning the phone rang and whenever Granny answered it she said things like, 'Hello, Anthea, no I haven't forgotten!' and 'Nothing can go wrong, Bob, because I have the cheese!'

And then Granny put down the phone and opened the fridge and took out two Black Bomber cheeses (which she must have bought when she was in Stonely yesterday). And then she popped them in her handbag.

'Armed and ready!' she said, giggling as she clicked

her bag closed, and all of a sudden she looked JUST like one of those criminals in films who laugh when they are about to commit a serious, true-life crime.

The phone rang again and this time we could tell it was the vicar because Granny said, 'Oh hello, vicar' (which was a bit of a giveaway) and then she said, 'Oh dear, what a bore for you. When did you last see it? Yes fine, I'll keep an eye out for it. Bye then.'

Granny sighed and raced around the house, making lists, popping things in her handbag and GETTING READY TO ROB A BANK.

We were so busy following her around that I kept forgetting to tell the others about my idea.

At 11:35 a.m. Granny told us it was time to leave because she wanted to make sure she could find a parking place in Stonely.

Just before we left, she asked if we'd seen her knitting bag, and we shook our heads and went bright red.

'Oh dear,' she said, searching under beds and behind

the curtains. 'What on earth have I done with it? Do tell me if you see it please, it's EXTREMELY important.' At that point I thought that maybe we should TELL Granny that we had hidden her balaclava in the weeping willow tree along with her stash of stolen money and new stripy top. But when I whispered this to the others, Tom ignored me and Pip twiddled her eyes (which is when they sort of go upside down and back to front) and Granny said, 'Stop twiddling your eyes, Pip,' and then she stopped asking about her knitting bag and told us to get our coats.

In Stonely, Granny parked on a side street and we walked towards the main Square. The town was busy because there is always a market on Saturday morning.

There were people with shopping bags and more cars than usual. When we crossed the High Street to go into the Square we nearly got run over by a blue van that drove right on to the curb.

'Hooligans!' said Granny, shaking her fist at the driver, but I pretended not to notice because when Granny shouts at strangers it's even more embarrassing than when Mum sends food back in restaurants.

We walked away from the blue van and came to the Square, which was just to our right. In the middle of the Square, towering over everything else, was a grand old building. On it was a sign that said 'Old Bank'.

'There it is!' said Tom pointing excitedly. At that point all I could do was swallow because I felt even more nervous than I do at the start of the 800 metres on Sports Day. Granny kept glancing from left to right as if she expected to see people and then she waved because Anthea was waiting outside the Old Bank.

'Ah,' said Anthea. 'I see you've brought the cavalry with you!'

We said hello to Anthea as normally as we could because Anthea used to be a spy and is good at spotting when people are up to something.

'You lot scrub up rather well, I must say,' said Anthea, nodding at our smart clothes. 'Well, spill the beans then,' she said, leaning towards us and chuckling. 'What's the latest? Any criminal gangs in our midst?'

I made a loud gulping sound and put my hand in my pocket and then I remembered what I had put in there

earlier this morning and I started breathing really loudly because I STILL hadn't managed to explain my plan to Tom and Pip.

'Oh good there's Janet!' said Anthea, pointing to Mrs Mackintosh who was walking towards us. 'Bang on time as usual! And isn't that Chris Norris on his bike?'

Chris Norris approached from the opposite direction. He nodded at Granny, Anthea and Mrs Mackintosh.

'Good morning, Chris!' said Granny cheerfully. 'Ready for lift off?'

Chris Norris smiled and nodded. I couldn't believe how calm and collected they were being.

'Goodo!' said Anthea. 'Then let's proceed. Bob is already inside, making the final preparations.' She glanced at her watch. 'Lift off is at twelve o'clock sharp. Comrades, the countdown begins.'

Granny told us we could run around in the Square for a few minutes because we usually do that in Stonely when she has errands to run.

'But come inside and find me at 12.05,' she said,

glancing at her watch. Anthea and Mrs Mackintosh gave each other a nod. They put their hands in their pockets and led Granny into the bank.

'Look!' said Tom. 'They're about to start the heist.'

But I didn't reply because at the same time, I spotted a police car parked up just outside the Old Bank. My heart went all wobbly because for one thing, I couldn't believe the police were already on to Granny's book club and for another thing, Granny didn't have a balaclava to hide her face – and it was OUR fault. Somehow, we had to find a way of distracting the police before they could witness Granny's robbery.

I put my hand in my pocket and wondered if this was as much of an emergency as the time when Max Smith fell off the climbing frame in the playground and landed on his head. Because when that happened I didn't have time to think, I just ran all the way to the park toilets because Max Smith's mum had gone there to change Max's little sister's nappy. And I shouted really loudly that Max had fallen off the climbing frame and Max Smith's mum called an ambulance on her mobile and later on, when Max was back home with his head stitched up, Max Smith's mum texted my mum and asked her to thank me for thinking on my feet in an emergency.

I decided that keeping the police away while Granny robbed a bank was even more of an emergency than Max Smith falling on his head. I took the red and yellow box of Fun Snaps out of my pocket and ran into the middle of the main Square. I opened the box and threw a handful of the tiny paper-covered Fun Snaps on to the paving slabs.

The noise that followed was what Mrs Vukovitch calls DEAFENING and what normal people say is PRETTY LOUD (because Mrs Vukovitch is prone to exaggeration).

BANG! BANG! BANG!

The Fun Snaps exploded as they hit the concrete. In London near where I live, the sound of Fun Snaps is not unusual. Where I live the police don't even CARE about

Fun Snaps because everybody knows that Fun Snaps aren't actually dangerous and you can buy them in the toy shop. But I could tell straightaway that the Stonely policeman DIDN'T know about Fun Snaps because the moment I threw that first handful, the front door of his police car opened and he raced out on to the street.

I threw another handful.

The policeman raced towards the Square AWAY FROM THE BANK and was immediately swallowed up in a large crowd of people who had come to investigate the banging noise.

'Nice one!' said Tom, as he and Pip caught up with me. 'Now we've just got to hope that Granny can finish robbing the bank before the policeman realises it's just a kid throwing Fun Snaps and goes back to his car.'

More shoppers and passers-by wandered over to the middle of the Square to find out what was making the banging sounds and the policeman walked around the crowds, pressing buttons on his walkie-talkie.

But then I ran out of Fun Snaps and everything went quiet again. The crowd of people started to walk away and the policeman spotted me holding an empty cardboard box. He put his walkie-talkie back in his belt and came over. 'Enough mucking around now, kid,' he said. 'You're creating a disturbance.' And then he walked back towards his car.

At the same time, I spotted Sally Merry walking through the front door of the Old Bank with her dog, Puff. I wondered what she was going to say when she discovered her husband and neighbours committing a bank robbery.

'We need a better diversion!' I said, wishing desperately that I had bought more boxes of Fun Snaps in my local toy shop last week.

Pip stared at the strangers wandering around and she looked at the policeman who was opening the door of his car. She took a deep breath.

'I have an idea,' she said and started to run across the Square. As soon as Pip had gained enough speed she launched herself into the air. She did a hand-spring, followed by a front flip, followed by a double somersault and, even though she was wearing uncomfortable dungarees with a baggy pocket across her tummy, she did them all perfectly.

'Good grief!' said a woman nearby. 'Have you seen that child?'

Pip did another run of four backflips and landed in the splits.

'Looks like the circus has come to town!' said a man, chuckling.

People started to wander back to the Square to watch Pip. They cheered and clapped and said things like, 'Crikey!' and 'Heavens above!'

The policeman noticed the crowd and wandered back into the Square to investigate.

'I thought she hated people watching her,' I said to Tom.

'She does,' said Tom proudly. 'But she'll do anything to stop Granny being arrested.'

I nodded and looked over at the Old Bank. Any minute now Granny and her book club would come out with their stash. If Pip could keep distracting the policeman they might be able to make a getaway without being seen. I started to think that everything might be OK.

But then I heard something that made my blood

turn cold and my heart race even faster than Pip's cartwheels. It was the sound of shouting and screaming and it wasn't coming from the crowd in the square, it was coming from inside the bank.

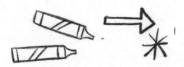

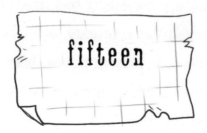

fifteen

I absolutely hate bad dreams. Sometimes when I have a bad dream at three in the morning, I get into Mum's bed and spend the rest of the night there. And even though I feel all wobbly from the badness of the dream, once I'm in Mum's bed I stop feeling frightened because everything is warm and safe and sometimes Mum smiles at me in her sleep.

But the screams inside the bank were way more frightening than my worst ever bad dream – especially when the policeman stopped watching Pip do backflips and started walking back towards the bank – and I couldn't hop into Mum's bed because I wasn't at home in London and Mum was at work AND NONE OF THIS WAS A DREAM. IT WAS REAL.

I could tell that something had gone wrong with Granny's bank robbery because a) it is not normal for bank robbers to spend that long inside doing the robbing and b) people only start screaming and shouting when things go wrong.

I looked at Tom and I knew he was scared too because he started taking really deep breaths.

The shouts and screams inside the bank got louder.

Pip stopped doing backflips and the policeman started to run.

'What's going on in there?' said Tom, trying not to look scared, even though his eyes were bulging.

'It might be a have-a-go hero?' said Pip breathlessly, coming to a sliding stop beside us.

'What's that?'

'It's when an innocent bystander risks life and limb to stop criminals carrying out a crime,' explained Tom. 'There's a have-a-go-hero in *Target!* She was a pensioner and she tripped up a gang of diamond thieves with her walking frame. She got a medal for bravery AND a

letter from the Queen.'

I was really interested in hearing more about this have-a-go-hero and finding out if the medal was made of solid gold, but at that exact moment Granny burst out of the bank. Her hair was crazy and her eyes looked blinky.

'Oh, there you are!' she shouted, waving at us. 'What on earth are you still doing out here? I asked you to meet me inside at 12.05. You've missed all the action.'

We ran towards her, nearly catching up with the policeman.

I don't remember EXACTLY what happened next because everything went REALLY fast and all I cared about was stopping Granny from being arrested for bank robbery.

'Granny!' I shouted, sprinting towards her and overtaking the policeman. 'The police are here. Make your getaway! Run for your life!'

I flung myself down on the ground in front of the policeman and tripped him up before he could reach

Granny. He landed on the pavement with a thud.

'By the cringe!' he said. 'What did you do that for?'

Tom and Pip caught up with me and sat down on top of the policeman. I looked out from under his armpit.

'Run!' I told Granny again. 'We'll deal with the police!'

But Granny did not make a getaway. She stared at us and she stared at the policeman lying on the pavement and she went all blinky.

The policeman tried to stand up. I kept tugging on his arm to pull him down again but he was really heavy. He heaved himself off the ground, spilling Tom and Pip onto the ground.

'Throw a Black Bomber at him!' I shouted at Granny. 'Hit him with it and run!'

'Why on earth would I want to do that?' said Granny.

'Don't worry, Granny!' said Pip, leaping up and racing towards her, 'I'll do it for you!'

Pip grabbed Granny's handbag and pulled out the two Black Bomber cheeses. She held one of them above her head and launched it at the policeman.

For a few seconds everything went into slow motion. The Black Bomber flew up into the air and seemed to stay up there for ages, a bit like Tom's frisbee on a windy day. Then it started to fall.

'For heaven's sake!' shouted Granny, glaring at Pip and rushing over to the policeman. 'Pip Berryman, stop that at once!'

Suddenly the world stopped travelling in slow

motion. Granny pushed the policeman out of the way and the Black Bomber cheese crashed on to the pavement. It shattered into a million cheesy pieces.

'I am SO sorry, Officer,' said Granny. 'These are my grandchildren and I think they must have got their wires crossed.'

Granny glared at us. 'As usual!' she said, crossly.

'I blimmin' hate cheese,' said the policeman, and Pip put the second Black Bomber into the baggy pocket of her dungarees. The policeman turned to me, Tom and Pip and asked us to explain ourselves 'pronto' (which by the way means right away).

At first, we concentrated hard on looking at the pavement because we didn't want to tell him about our own grandmother being a bank robber, but Granny

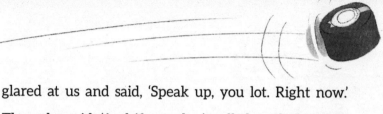

glared at us and said, 'Speak up, you lot. Right now.' Then she said, 'And if you don't tell the whole truth, you will be in even bigger trouble'. So we had to tell the policeman EVERYTHING because even though we didn't want to snitch, it is against the law to lie to a policeman, especially one you have tripped up and thrown cheddar cheese at.

So I started at the beginning and told the policeman about reading the article about the Stonely Robbers and how they were hiding in one of the nearby villages. I told him about the blood on Chris Norris's shirt, and how he had a massive rucksack and a shed full of stolen paintings, and I told him about Granny's book club not talking about books once for the whole entire evening. I mentioned the red balaclava we found in Granny's knitting bag, and about how Granny herself told us that Black Bomber cheddar is a lethal weapon. I explained about how Granny and her friends are always short of money and trying to save electricity etc. Finally, I talked for a long time about what a good woman our granny is and how she didn't mean to rob banks, she was just a bit short of cash, especially because the vicar was always asking her for money for a new church roof. And Tom and Pip nodded and looked at their shoes. The whole time I was talking, Granny's mouth fell wide open.

The only thing I forgot to mention was the stash of money we'd found in Granny's front garden and hidden in the weeping willow tree, but by the time I remembered about it the policeman had asked if I was finished and I said, 'Yes,' because my mouth was getting dry from talking so much.

'See that building there,' said the policeman, 'the one you say is a bank?'

I nodded.

'Used to be a bank,' he said, in a not-very-kind voice. 'USED TO BE. Until about twenty years ago when it was turned into a posh restaurant. Hence the name: OLD Bank. The real bank is over there.' He pointed to a building on the High Street.

We all went a bit quiet and gulpy and for the first time I started to wonder if, maybe, something had gone ever so slightly wrong in our investigation.

'Madam,' he said, turning to Granny. 'I'm really sorry but I'm afraid I have to follow things up. Firstly, have you just been carrying out a robbery in the Old Bank restaurant?'

Granny snorted.

'Of course I haven't,' she said. 'I've been helping to organise a surprise seventieth birthday party for my next-door neighbour, Sally Merry. That's the top-secret plan we've been trying to keep quiet. We've been planning it for weeks and we arranged everything during our book club meetings so Sally wouldn't get suspicious. Then, yesterday, we popped into Stonely

to make sure everything was ready for the party. And this morning, Bob told Sally he was taking her for a birthday lunch, just the two of them, and we were all here, waiting to surprise her! That's what the clapping and screaming was about. We were shouting "Surprise!" at the tops of our lungs.'

Granny shook her head. 'The reason I didn't tell my grandchildren about any of this is because I didn't trust them to keep their mouths shut. I wonder why!'

Tom and Pip suddenly seemed REALLY interested in a piece of chewing gum stuck to a drain.

'But what about the balaclava you're knitting?' I said, quietly.

'Balaclava?' said Granny. 'What balaclava?'

'The red thing in your knitting bag with the two eye holes.'

Granny made a face. 'That's not a balaclava!' she spluttered. 'That's a dog jumper for Puff, Sally Merry's poodle. I've been knitting it for her birthday.'

'And the stripy top in your cupboard?' I whispered.

'I bought it to wear to Sally's party!' said Granny crossly. 'Not because I was planning to commit a bank heist.'

Tom cleared his throat.

'But Chris Norris DID have blood on his shirt and he also had a massive rucksack and he definitely had a shed full of stolen paintings,' he said. 'And the police put out a statement saying that the criminals were probably hiding out in an old shed. It says so here.' Tom pulled out the crumpled newspaper article and showed it to Granny and the policeman.

Granny read the article and gave the policeman a sideways look.

'It wasn't BLOOD on his shirt, it was paint. He's always covered in the stuff.' She turned to face the policeman. 'And that shed up by the allotments? That's his art studio. Chris Norris is a famous artist.'

She shook her head and turned back to us. 'Chris Norris has been working on a surprise painting for Sally's birthday. Bob commissioned him. That's why you saw him at my house, he was delivering the painting. But Bob hasn't given it to Sally yet,' Granny hissed. 'So don't you dare spoil the surprise!'

Granny paused and turned to the policeman. 'It's a beautiful painting,' she said.

'The only paintings I'm interesting in,' he said, shaking his head, 'are stolen ones.'

For a second, I thought that maybe Granny had forgiven us, but then she narrowed her eyes and said, 'Honestly!' in a really cross voice.

I chewed my lip. I couldn't believe we had got it so wrong. Granny and her friends weren't the bank robbers and Chris Norris was a famous artist. I remembered about Sally Merry telling us it was her seventieth birthday on Saturday. It suddenly all made sense.

'Right,' said Granny. 'Apologise to this poor policeman at once and, then, please can we all go back into the Old Bank and help Sally Merry celebrate her birthday.'

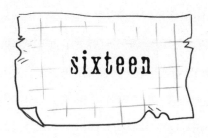

sixteen

Sally Merry's surprise seventieth birthday was mainly full of people who lived in Muddlemoor and Stonely and other nearby villages. I didn't know all of them but I recognised quite a few, like for instance, the whole of Granny's book club and Chris Norris and Mrs Rooney from the village shop who kept checking her watch because she isn't used to closing the shop on a Saturday afternoon. Ronnie Mehta was by the bar, eating crisps and chatting on his phone but there was no sign of Rupi and Nina.

Sally kept saying, 'I had no idea!' and 'What a lovely surprise!' and Bob wouldn't stop smiling because he was so happy the surprise had worked. Their poodle Puff barked and jumped up at people but even though

some people didn't like it, Sally and Bob just laughed.

Bob turned to me, Tom and Pip and said, 'Did you scallywags guess what we were up to?' and we had to shake our heads and say, 'No,' because we couldn't exactly tell him the truth, i.e. that we'd thought he was a bank robber.

Occasionally, Granny wandered over to us. 'Just checking you're not accusing some other poor OAP of heinous crimes,' she said under her breath. Except we didn't laugh because it wasn't funny.

Granny invited the policeman to stay for a cup of tea and he said, 'I might just do that, I'm a bit shaken up after that kerfuffle with the cheese.' And Granny made us apologise to him AGAIN and she also told us she wanted to have a little chat with us, and our hearts went all sinky because when grown-ups want a 'little chat' they normally just want to tell you off.

Granny told us that although SHE could cope with being accused of being a bank robber we had to stop going around accusing her friends. 'One day,' she said, frowning at us, 'you are going to get somebody in REAL trouble.'

I nodded because saying nothing can be safer than spilling the beans but Tom, who likes to have the last word, said, 'We were actually trying to stop YOU getting in trouble.' Granny rolled her eyes and said, 'I mean it, Tom!' and then she told us to stay out of trouble because she didn't want anything else ruining Sally's birthday party.

After that we found a sofa in the corner and sat down with a bowl of barbecue crisps. None of us said much because we were REALLY disappointed that we had failed to track down the real Stonely Robbers.

'They're still on the loose,' said Tom sadly. 'We've failed.' And I knew that Tom minded about this A LOT because one thing he doesn't like to do in life is fail.

A long time went by and eventually Pip whispered that she felt a bit dizzy and then Tom explained that, last Christmas, Pip fainted in the school carol service because of having to sit still for sixty-seven minutes.

I said, 'Pip, are you in danger of fainting?' and Pip said, 'Possibly,' and that's when I suggested we get out of that room right away to avoid having a medical emergency on our hands.

We got down on our hands and knees and crawled out of the Old Bank because we didn't want Granny to spot us leaving. Crawling was quite tricky because there were a lot of legs and walking sticks in our way and some people were wearing high heels, but when

we got to the door we managed to sneak through it without anyone noticing.

The streets of Stonely were much quieter now because all the market stalls were being packed away. We stood next to the empty police car and Pip took loads of deep breaths and eventually she stopped feeling dizzy and said, 'I think I might be allergic to seventieth birthday parties,' and I nodded because I knew exactly what she meant.

Tom said that we'd all had a big shock to our systems and when you have a shock to your system you need to eat sugar to recover. Tom said this was medically proven to be true and if we didn't believe him we could ask his science teacher, Mrs Aidley. Pip pointed out that we couldn't exactly ask Mrs Aidley now because we weren't anywhere near their school in Wales, but Tom ignored Pip and said he had just remembered about a really good sweet shop on the High Street next to the cinema. Then Tom started walking down the High Street towards the sweet shop and me and Pip followed him.

We walked straight past the blue van that had nearly run us over earlier and Tom said, 'Hooligans!' in his best Granny voice, and me and Pip giggled. I started to feel a bit better about everything because I realised that it was actually a good thing that Granny WASN'T a bank robber, and even though visiting Granny in prison would have been more interesting than going to a seventieth birthday party, it would also have been quite sad.

I started humming and Pip did a one-handed cartwheel and Tom talked non-stop about Fruit Pastilles and strawberry laces but then, when he was in the middle of telling us how to make a fake strawberry flavouring out of chemicals (which he had read about in one of his science books), Tom stopped talking and made a weird yelping sound. At first, I thought he'd been stung by something, e.g. a hornet (because hornets are even worse than wasps) but then he stopped yelping and I knew he hadn't been stung because he wasn't crying and making a MASSIVE fuss, which is what Tom always does when he gets hurt or injured or sees the sight of blood.

Tom pulled me and Pip down behind a large motorbike and Pip said, 'Ouch,' and Tom said, 'Look!' and pointed at the blue van. Coming out of it were five people in red balaclavas. They were carrying large empty rucksacks and were running towards the bank on the High Street.

Tom's teeth started chattering under his breath but Pip didn't make a sound because even when she is in a life-threatening situation, e.g. surrounded by a gang of people in red balaclavas, she doesn't make a fuss. I took a massive breath and my legs went wobbly because you didn't have to be a genius to realise that the people in red balaclavas and rucksacks were the REAL STONELY ROBBERS and they were on their way to rob a REAL BANK.

The next few minutes were a confusing blur because everything happened in fast forward. It was a bit like when I spin my school PE bag round really, really quickly so it stops looking like a PE bag and is more like a fuzzy green bush. Luckily the motorbike

we were hiding behind was MASSIVE so the robbers didn't spot us. A man with a deep voice said, 'Three minutes to get the loot!' and then all five robbers burst through the door of the bank.

'We need to get the police pronto,' Tom whispered, and before me or Pip could say one single word, Tom said that HE should be the one to run back to the Old Bank to alert the policeman because he was the fastest runner.

Tom told me and Pip to stop the robbers from making a getaway, but when I asked him how exactly we were meant to do that he started hyperventilating and running very fast towards the Square.

For a few seconds, everything felt really quiet.

'We need to stop them getting away before the police get here,' said Pip, and I just nodded because I could hear muffled shouts coming from inside the bank and true-life words wouldn't come out of my mouth. We both stared at the back of the van.

Tom had only just reached the door of the Old Bank. Any minute now the robbers would come out of the real bank, jump into the van and make their getaway. We were running out of time. I looked at the van's exhaust pipe and turned to face Pip. At that point a million thoughts began swirling into my head until I felt really DIZZY and a bit sick. 'I have an idea,' I said, 'but it may be the most dangerous thing we have ever done in our lives and also it might not even work.'

I told Pip about Mum's car breaking down on the way to Granny's because the exhaust pipe was full of sycamore leaves and then I said, 'Why don't we try to block the van's exhaust because that might stop the robbers driving away?'

Straightaway Pip said, 'That's a really good idea,' but then she said, 'What can we use to block it?' and I went bright red because I hadn't thought about that.

I looked around for some leaves or stones or even an old coke can to put in the van's exhaust pipe but the pavements in Stonely were really clean and tidy – not at all like the ones in London.

'Sorry,' I said. 'It's not a very good idea after all.' But Pip told me to hang on and then she put her hand in the big pocket of her dungarees and finally she smiled at me. 'Will this work?' she said, pulling out the second Black Bomber cheese.

The door of the bank shuddered and the shouts inside got louder. This was our only chance.

Pip handed the Black Bomber to me and I crept out from behind the motorbike. I took a step forward and tried to push the cheese into the van's exhaust pipe.

It wouldn't fit. Pip crept out from behind the motorbike to help. She squeezed while I pushed. The door of the bank flew open.

'Last try!' gasped Pip and this time we pushed the cheese so hard that the black wax casing caught on a sharp bit of the exhaust and started to peel away. The round ball of cheddar inside was soft and easy to mould. I squeezed it into a sausage shape and pushed really hard until it started sliding effortlessly into the narrow pipe.

Pip and I fell backwards onto the pavement just as the robbers started running towards their van. As we flung ourselves back behind the motorbike I thought I could hear Pip's heart thumping through her clothes.

The robbers opened the back doors of the van and threw in their loaded rucksacks. Two of them – a man and woman – leaped in after the rucksacks and slammed the doors shut. The other three, including the driver with the loud voice, climbed up behind the steering wheel. I heard the key turn in the ignition and me and Pip clutched each other, waiting to see if our plan had worked.

But instead of breaking down like Mum's car did, the van's engine roared into life and the robbers drove off at top speed.

I felt even more disappointed than the time I got the Norovirus and had to miss the class trip to Legoland.

'Never mind,' said Pip, putting her arm round me. 'At least we tried.' I shrugged and at the same time I spotted Tom charging towards us,

followed by the police officer.

'Where are the robbers?' he shouted. 'I've called for back-up.'

I pointed at the van. It was beeping its horn angrily at a traffic jam at the end of the High Street. I explained how we'd tried to break the van's engine by blocking the exhaust with a Black Bomber cheese but that it hadn't worked, and then I stopped talking because I was a bit embarrassed.

'Not MORE blinking cheese,' said the police officer, shaking his head.

At that point, Granny and Anthea appeared and we had to explain everything all over again really fast. Granny made her eyes go all narrow and staring, and even though me and Pip said sorry over and over again I could tell she was really worried because she kept hugging us and saying, 'You might have been BADLY hurt,' in a really cross voice.

But Anthea didn't look cross or worried because she was busy staring at the back of the blue van which was now trying to overtake the traffic by driving on to the pavement. 'Black Bomber cheese,' she said, chuckling. 'That should do the jo—' and before she'd even finished her sentence we heard a MASSIVE bang and the blue van stopped in the middle of the pavement.

'Gotcha!' said Anthea, setting off down the High Street.

'Well I never!' said the police officer, racing after Anthea and blowing his whistle.

Me, Tom, Pip and Granny set off after them as more police cars screeched up. The blue van was surrounded by thick black smoke and there was a strong smell of cheese. Inside the van, the Stonely Robbers were shouting loudly. The driver opened the door and saw us running towards him. He said a lot of really rude words – too rude to put in this story – and then he leaped out on to the pavement and started to run away.

'Come along, Sergeant,' said Anthea, giving the policeman a nudge. 'I think you have some arresting to do.'

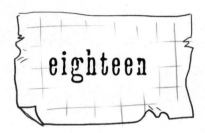

eighteen

The Stonely Robbers were taken away in separate police cars. Anthea told us we had showed great determination and initiative. 'Two things they can't teach in those schools of yours,' she said, patting us on the back.

Even Granny stopped being cross and worried and said she was 'EXTREMELY proud.'

More amazingly, the policeman forgave us for tripping him up and throwing cheese at him, and actually thanked us for our help.

A few minutes later, a local newspaper reporter turned up on her bicycle to interview us for a story in the next day's newspaper. Tom did most of the talking, but I told her the bit about blocking the van's exhaust pipe with a Black Bomber cheese.

When the interview was over, Granny and Anthea took us back to the Old Bank. None of the other party guests had a clue what we had been up to, and Granny said it was probably best they didn't find out because it might ruin the party atmosphere. We arrived back just in time to hear Sally Merry make a birthday speech.

Sally thanked everybody for coming and then she thanked Granny's book club for planning the party so brilliantly. 'I absolutely LOVE surprises!' she said, all happy. Then she said something in Italian (because one of her favourite hobbies is Italian lessons in the village hall with a Scottish teacher called Mario).

When Sally had finished making her speech, Bob stood up and spoke about all the things Sally had done in her life except I can't remember what they were because when it comes to speeches, I find it quite hard to listen.

After that, Bob told Sally it was time for her to open her present and he took a square parcel out of Chris

Norris's huge blue rucksack. Sally opened the parcel and inside was a painting with lots of lines and dashes on it. Bob told Sally it was of their house in Italy and Sally squealed because she was so happy. She thanked Chris Norris and Chris Norris said it was a pleasure. I looked carefully at Chris Norris's shirt to see if I could see the blood except it didn't look like blood anymore, it looked like red paint.

Everybody cheered and said that Chris Norris's painting was 'magnificent' and 'marvellous' except I could have done a better painting myself and I'm not even very good at art.

Eventually, Bob and Sally stopped talking and told everybody to finish off the puddings because it was nearly time to go home. 'There should be some cheese too,' said Bob, 'but I don't know where it's got to.'

I glanced at Tom and Pip, and they glanced back and then we headed to the pudding table before we had to start explaining about where the cheese had got to.

'Tuck in, kiddos,' said Anthea, joining us. 'All that detective work must have given you an appetite.'

We nodded because our mouths were so full of chocolate roulade we couldn't actually speak.

'Talking of detective work,' said Anthea. 'I don't suppose you've seen the vicar's cash box, have you? I was just talking to him and he is most agitated because he still hasn't found the church funds.'

I stopped eating chocolate roulade and I slightly

spluttered and I glanced at Tom and Pip to see if they were thinking what I was thinking, i.e. about the cash box we had found yesterday and hidden in the weeping willow tree in Ronnie Mehta's garden.

'You'd think,' said Anthea, fixing us with a very long stare, 'that in a safe, trusting place like Muddlemoor, SOMEBODY would have found the vicar's cash box and returned it to him at the vicarage.'

Pip made a loud squeaking sound and Tom spat out a bit of chocolate roulade and we all tried really hard not to go bright red.

'Anyway!' boomed Anthea, giving us another long look. 'I'm sure you'll let the vicar know if you happen to find that cash of his hidden in some unusual place.'

We waited for Anthea to go and then we raced over to Granny and I said, 'Can you drive us back to

Muddlemoor right now please, Granny, because there is something really important we have to do.'

Granny stopped drinking her cup of tea and stared at us.

'May I ask what this important thing is?' she said. and Tom said, 'I'm afraid not because it's classified information,' and Granny snorted through her nose and said, 'Spill the beans or I won't drive you back to Muddlemoor!' And I could tell she meant business because she put her hands on her hips.

So we ended up having to tell Granny about the mix up with the vicar's missing cash and how we had hidden it in Ronnie Mehta's weeping willow tree BY MISTAKE. And then I couldn't help pointing out that Rupi and Nina Mehta had seen us coming out of the weeping willow tree yesterday, just after we had hidden the money there, and that I was a bit worried they might try to steal the vicar's money for themselves because they needed loads of money for a trip to Rwanda.

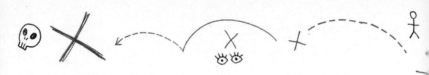

Granny waited until I'd finished and then stared at us for a long time with a crinkly expression on her face.

Eventually she said, 'You are not to go round accusing lovely people like Rupi and Nina Mehta of stealing!' Then she frowned quite a lot and said, 'As for the poor vicar!'

'Does that mean you'll drive us back to Muddlemoor?' Tom asked.

Granny picked up her handbag and said, 'Do I have a choice?'

And Tom said, 'Not really because I think the vicar is really worried about his missing money.'

We all watched the vicar leaving the party with an anxious look on his face and Granny sighed and rummaged in her handbag for her car key.

'But this is the last time you involve me in one of your capers,' she said.

I gave Granny a reassuring pat on the back and told her not to worry because worrying isn't good for old people's rickety hearts and this made Granny giggle and then she giggled a bit more and then we all started giggling (because it's hard not to giggle when somebody else is) and then we couldn't stop.

We were still in hysterics when we arrived back at Little Draycott. We didn't go into Granny's house. Instead, we went to Ronnie Mehta's and cut through a side path straight into his back garden. When we reached the weeping willow tree, Granny said, 'So this is where all the plotting takes place!' and we didn't say anything because we didn't want to give up our secrets in broad daylight. Me, Tom and Pip crept inside the weeping willow tree, and for a few seconds everything went very quiet but then we all breathed MASSIVE sighs of relief because the cash box was still there, hidden underneath Granny's new stripy top and a pile of red knitting.

We came out and showed everything to Granny and she stopped laughing and went back to being slightly cross. 'Children,' she said, 'you have to stop taking things that aren't yours.'

We said sorry AGAIN and then I asked Granny if we could run to the vicarage straightaway to give the vicar back his money before anyone else, e.g. Rupi and Nina Mehta, got their hands on it. But Granny snorted and said that SHE would come with us to take the money back to the vicar because right now she didn't trust us as far as she could throw us. So after that we piled into Granny's car and drove through the village towards the church.

We went past the playground and the village hall and the big house on the corner and we saw lots of people arriving back from Sally Merry's seventieth birthday party. The sun was shining and there was a gentle breeze. Even though a lot had happened to us that day, it was just a normal afternoon for most people in Muddlemoor.

I suddenly felt really tired.

'What does Albie Short do when an investigation ends?' I asked, yawning. I was slightly hoping that maybe Albie Short liked playing Lego when he wasn't tracking down dangerous criminals.

'He doesn't rest,' said Tom. 'As soon as one investigation finishes, he moves on to the next one. That's the thing about detectives.'

'Hmmm,' said Granny, chuckling as she parked her car outside the vicarage and set off up the front path. 'Well in that case, I think I'd better keep a MUCH closer eye on you lot from now on.'

I got a bit worried about this because I didn't like the idea of Granny checking up on us every time we stayed with her in Muddlemoor. But when the vicar answered the door, Granny forgot to tell him the truth about how we had accidentally stolen his money, and that's when I remembered that when it comes to keeping an eye on us, Granny is mainly quite forgetful. After that I felt a lot better.

The vicar was so pleased to have his money back he didn't ask us any tricky questions. He invited us all in for tea and when we got fidgety he didn't make us run round in the garden like most grown-ups do, he told us we could turn on the telly. So we did. And it was really good timing because *Ninja Heroes* was just starting and we watched it all the way to the end.

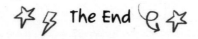 The End